YOU'RE THE ROGUE THAT I WANT

ROGUES OF REDMERE BOOK 1

SAMANTHA HOLT

CHAPTER ONE

ornwall, England 1811
     Red spat out another mouthful of salty water. The sea spray struck him across the face, bitter and unpleasant. Waves rolled in, sloshing over the edges of his boots and filling them. He grimaced. The seas were particularly rough tonight. They'd be lucky to haul in all the goods before sunrise. His muscles burned as he dragged what had to be the tenth keg of the night to shore.

Cold wind slapped his face and ruffled his shirt. Through his teeth, he cursed the unpredictable English weather. Though, truth be told, they'd dealt with worse. However, considering the mood he was in tonight, he did not much fancy dealing with anything other than a shot of whiskey. Some days he wondered what possessed him to drag his arse out in the middle of the night and fight the weather—and sometimes the local excise men—all in the name of a profit.

Beside him, two other men worked hard to fight the waves and ensure their cargo was not lost. Frosty ribbons of moonlight glinted off the white tips of the waves farther out.

The rowboats that had been used to bring in the goods were long since stowed away, and the ship would be headed to the docks.

As another strong wave nearly toppled him, he muttered what could perhaps have been conceived as sarcastic thanks. At least they had avoided the worst of it when rowing in, but could that damned wind have not waited until after they'd brought in their haul?

Red glanced over at Knight, who worked a darned sight faster than he or Nate. Of course, the muscle-bound man had quite the advantage over them and seemed to cut through the waves like a frigate.

"Nearly done," Knight declared over the wind, hefting a trunk onto the cart.

Red pushed his sodden hair from his face with one hand and dragged the cask out of the sea by the fishing net. He paused to squint into the sea. Once upon a time they had been able to unload their cargo in broad daylight while the weather was calm, but the customs men had increased their patrols of late. Red and his crew had been forced to become sneakier.

Nate brought in what looked to be the last keg and paused to take a breath. "At least it isn't raining," he said with a grin.

"That's all of them?" Red asked.

They all paused to study the surf as it churned and bubbled. Their haul had been left in fishermen's nets just past where the waves broke. The nets could be spotted easily enough in the light, but the knotted floats were not so easy to spy in the inky ocean at night. However, their new method of bringing smuggled goods in from France was worth it. It gave them time to bring in the cargo—and time, they had discovered, could be vitally important when it came to the customs men.

"Let's get this stowed away before we get any wetter. I have a hankering for a whiskey."

Nate chuckled. "When do you not?"

Red grunted at this. "Don't be jealous of my finer tastes. You'll enjoy the nicer things in life one day—once your balls have dropped."

Nate, only two years his junior and his brother, laughed again. Knight clapped him hard on the shoulder, and Red saw Nate wince. Sometimes the giant of a man seemed to forget he was twice the size of them all.

"We had better get moving. Louisa said the excise men had already been in tonight." Knight nodded to the cart.

Red nodded. "Hopefully that means they have been and gone but—"

"They're sneaky bastards," finished Nate.

"Yes," he agreed. He let a grin break across his face. "But we are sneakier."

They all chuckled. After he and Nate clambered onto the cart, he took the reins and urged the horses forward. With the help of a push from the behemoth that was Knight, they eased the vehicle off the stony shore and onto the grass. Knight walked behind them until they hit the dirt tracks and then he climbed onto the cart. He understood well enough that they could do without his extra weight until they were on the roads.

Red directed the wagon along the narrow track until the hedgerows grew close. The road itself could hardly be considered a road—more like a dirt track—and was impassable when it rained. On days like those they were forced to bring in the haul on foot, stowing it in a cave not far from their landing spot until the path dried out.

He shuddered, aware of water still sloshing about in his boots. As much as the cursed wind made life difficult, Nate had been right. The rain would have made their job twenty times harder and their last lot of cargo had been a bother to bring in when they'd been struck by a downpour.

Christ, he longed for the days when they could bring in their goods with as much ease as a merchant man.

Once they reached the barn, he paused to drag on his greatcoat.

"Cold?" Nate asked.

"Damned right I am."

"It's that noble blood of yours," he said with a smirk.

"Yours is the same," Red muttered.

"I'm plenty warm," Knight remarked.

They both glanced at him. Red shook his head. Knight could not fail to be warm with the bulk of him. He suspected the man could stand out in the snow for two weeks and be perfectly content. He'd never met a man so hardy, and in their business, it was quite the asset.

They opened the back of the cart, and Red unlocked the barn door. "Put the wine near the door," he ordered. "It will not be there long."

Knight nodded and began unloading with a swift ease that made Red feel like a crippled old man, in spite of Knight being potentially older than him. At least they thought so. No one really knew, not even Knight.

Red stilled. He motioned to the men to do the same. Breath held, he listened.

"Horses," Nate whispered.

He nodded. "Open both the doors, we'll put the cart inside."

Knight and Nate pulled them open and he urged the horses into the dark confines of the barn. Thankfully they had little left of their last haul or else it would never have fit in along with the horses. He clambered off quickly and locked the barn door behind him.

All three of them were well-rehearsed in dodging the excise men or any potentially nosey strangers. The rugged Cornish countryside provided plenty of hiding spots, and they tucked themselves behind a crumbling stone wall.

The sound of horse hooves neared. Collectively they held their breaths. Should the revenue men come upon them, they would be nothing more than three drunken men, lost on their way home from the inn. But it would be enough to arouse suspicion and potentially search the barn. None of them wanted that.

Red twisted his head enough to view the horses and their riders as they belted past. Three of them, well-dressed. Excise men to be sure. He cursed inwardly. They were becoming more determined.

They waited until the patrol was long gone before moving from their spot. A curse from Nate drew his attention.

"What is—" Red laughed as he spotted a sheep determinedly butting into Nate's leg. He must have come from a nearby field and had apparently taking a liking to his brother. "Looks like you've made a friend."

"Or an enemy," Nate grumbled when the animal retreated and came at him again. Nate held up his hands to try to stop the animal from coming near but the white, grubby-looking sheep was determined to butt into his leg. In spite of clapping his hands and stomping his feet, the animal continued forward before coming to a stop and giving him a gentler nudge.

"She likes you," Knight said.

"Come, let us finish our work here and leave Nate's friend in peace. Then I can have a damned whiskey."

"It is *not* my friend," Nate protested as they opened the barn to continue unloading.

The damned sheep followed them into the barn.

Red shook his head. Nothing about tonight had gone smoothly.

CHAPTER TWO

"Oh." Hannah tried to tug the hem of her pelisse out from under the boot—*the extremely muddy boot*—of a short but heavy man. "P-pardon me."

The short man ignored her, too deep into his cups and the conversation he was having with his friends in the entrance to the inn. She gave another tug and heard a frightful ripping sound. She stumbled forward and her palms struck something warm and solid. Hannah jerked back and lifted her gaze to the mammoth of a man. A scar upon his lip, shoulders worthy of a fairytale giant and dark, dark eyes. A tremble racked her.

"F-forgive me."

He merely peered at her as though she was some strange creature from the deep. She might as well be, she concluded. She did not belong in this crowded inn, late at night, amongst drunks and gamblers.

Resisting the urge to draw out her handkerchief and place it to her nose, she took several steps back. It was not that the giant smelled—no it was more the general odor of the place that had her wrinkling her nose. In fact, he had been about the cleanest smelling man she had encountered so far. He folded his arms and frowned at her, forcing her to take a few more steps back, only for her to strike someone else.

This person did notice her and took particular exception to her knocking into his ale. She was none too pleased to have done so either, not when it sloshed over the back of her coat. She twisted her face as a trickle of the cold drink seeped under her collar and slid down her back.

"Clumsy girl," the owner of the ale muttered.

"I am sorry," she said, easing away from the glowering man.

She ignored the giant and pushed deeper into the crowded confines of the inn. Hannah tried not to pass judgement on the patrons—after all, she was hardly an ill-traveled woman and had seen worse places—but none of them did anything to dissuade her initial impression of them.

On several small round tables, tucked into the alcove windows, games of cards were taking place with money being lost and won. She ducked under a wooden beam and stepped around a drunken man sprawled half upon the floor, his back propped up against the bar.

Hannah gripped her pelisse about her and pushed her way through to the bar, placing a hand on the worn wood only to draw it straight back as she came into contact with something sticky and indescribable. She tried to catch the eye of a barmaid, but the woman was too busy dashing about, her tray laden with pints of ale.

Tears threatened to burn in her eyes. She sniffed them back and blinked them away. *No tears, my girl*, her father's voice intoned.

"No tears," she muttered, recalling the many, many times her father said farewell as he went off on expeditions. She had held back the tears then; she could certainly hold them back now. Goodness, she could hardly stand in the middle of a busy inn and blub now, could she?

It was merely exhaustion. Yes, that was it. It had been a long trip on the mail coach. She had not been able to catch it from Falmouth until seven in the evening. It had been preferable to a stage coach as it was less busy and quicker. Her father always took the mail coach when given the option and his letter had urged her to make haste. The problem was, it was far past time she should be in bed, and she had eaten no supper. Her stomach grumbled, her bottom hurt from being bounced about inside the coach, and a slight headache was starting up.

She glanced around and saw the serving girl heading her way once more. Drawing up her shoulders, she stepped deliberately in front of the girl. With a pretty face, dark, golden hair and a generous bust, Hannah imagined the girl was good for business. If the looks she was getting were any indication, Hannah's supposition was correct.

The girl glanced her over, most likely noting how out of place she was.

"E-excuse me," Hannah started.

"Yes?" Someone behind her bellowed for another ale, and she waved away the customer. "Are you lost, love?"

"N-no, I'm looking for someone." She leaned in. "His name is Red." She whispered the last part.

"What do you want with him?"

"I need to speak with him. It's an urgent matter."

The woman shrugged. "He is over there." She motioned to a lone table tucked by the fireplace. Shadows shielded her from seeing the face of the man but sure enough, she could see a figure hunched over a drink, the firelight picking out only his shaggy hair and the glass of amber liquid in his hand. "Be careful," the serving girl warned, "he's not in the best of moods."

Hannah smirked to herself. She had dealt with much this past week, travelling alone from Hampshire to Cornwall. A grumpy man could hardly intimidate her.

"Thank you."

She made her way over to the man who appeared determined to ignore everything and everyone. She noted the bottle of whiskey on his table—a fine brand that her father sometimes enjoyed. At least half of it was missing. Hopefully he was not too inebriated.

"Excuse me," she started but her voice came out like nothing more than a mouse's squeak. She coughed and tried again. "Excuse me, are you Red?"

His head jerked up. "Who wants to know?"

She took another step closer and gasped. The firelight cleared the shadows around his features. She was not sure what she expected from an infamous smuggler but it was not this. Where were the pock marks? The scars? The missing teeth?

There were no missing teeth to be sure. Though he kept his mouth in a firm line of disdain—or perhaps annoyance— the quick flash she had seen had revealed a mouth of perfectly healthy teeth. As for scars or pockmarks, his skin was perfect.

His light brown hair was, admittedly, a little too long and his face was unshaven, revealing several days of neglect. There were shadows around his eyes too, and he looked weary. However, that could not take away from that fact he was a handsome man.

He stared at her expectantly. She gulped. "I need your help."

"And if I do not wish to give it?"

She shook her head. Impossible. He had to help her. He was her only chance. She dragged out the chair opposite and sat. One dark brow rose at the action. Chin lifted, she propped her arms on the table and leaned forward. He smelled of the sea.

"I need your help bringing across something from France. I'm told you are the man for the job."

"Then you were told wrong."

"I can pay handsomely."

"I don't need coin."

"Do you not? I thought all smugglers did."

He leaned forward abruptly. "You need to watch your tongue, miss." He glanced around. "Not everyone here is a friend."

She jerked back a little. Handsome he might be, but he was also intimidating. His strong jaw, finished with a slight dip that was just visible under the stubble, was set firmly. His eyes glinted in the firelight though she could not tell their color properly.

She took a breath and cast her gaze over him. It was something she was in the habit of doing. Study everything closely enough and any fear she might have of it left. It had worked with spiders. When one looked closely, one could see they were no more than a few legs and a body pieced together. Those long legs no longer appeared so terrifying once she had seen them under a microscope and appreciated the unique design of the creatures.

It did not seem to quite work with this creature. His slightly creased forehead and the still lifted brow did not lose any of it sternness. His lips, she concluded, were generous for a man's, but it did not soften his appearance. She pictured him in evening wear and that helped a little, though she could tell he would be ridiculously handsome and likely still no more polite.

"I was told you were the man to help me," she said, aware of being a little breathless.

"As I said, you were told wrong."

"Will you not even listen to what I need your help with?"

He leaned back and pushed a hand through his hair before folding his arms across a wide chest. Not as wide as the giant's for certain but wide enough to tell her he could break her in half with ease. She had to wonder what she had been thinking coming here but she had no choice.

"Miss..."

"Hannah St. John."

"Miss St. John. I am tired and cold. I have had a long evening. I have no wish to hear tales of damsels in distress. I suggest you find someone who enjoys tales of woe because I, for one, do not."

"I am no damsel in distress."

"Really? Could have fooled me."

"You say you are tired. I have travelled many miles to come to see you. I have been awake for far longer than I should have been. I have not eaten all day and have walked on foot, across unknown countryside, in the dark, to find you. I am not sure how that makes me a damsel or in distress, but it certainly makes me as tired and impatient as you. If you would give me but a moment, I could make my case and leave you to your drink." She glanced at it in distaste. "No doubt you wish to find the bottom of the bottle."

Red chuckled, the sound low and oddly appealing. His gaze never leaving hers, he poured another glass full of the liquid and threw it back before refilling his glass.

She pursed her lips. "My father says you should savor Greybeard whisky."

"Your father is a smart man. And I would be savoring it quite nicely had I not been interrupted."

"Listen to my offer, and I will leave you in peace," she pressed.

His smile grew narrow. Red cradled his glass of whiskey, rolling it around the glass so that it left a coating on the inside. She watched the drink glide back down the inside of the glass.

"Very well then. I shall listen, I shall tell you no, and you —" he thrust a thumb toward the door "—shall leave."

She didn't challenge him. Surely when he heard her tale he would wish to help? Who would not want to be part of history in the making?

"I need something bringing over from France."

"Yes, you said as much."

"There is no need to be rude."

"There is every need. I hardly think you were considering manners when you interrupted my peaceful drink."

She opened her mouth, snapped it shut and drew in a long breath. "Anyway, I have to get this object from here to London. It is imperative it gets there safely without anyone knowing."

"It must be a valuable object."

"It is."

"Why not get someone in Portsmouth or Southampton to bring it over? Why not hop on a ship yourself?"

"You must know how impossible it is with the war. And Portsmouth and Southampton are too closely controlled. My father explicitly told me to bring it to Cornwall. Even Kent is too dangerous. Did you not hear of that smuggling ring that were rounded up and hanged recently?"

He shrugged. "I heard murmurings."

"It does not frighten you?"

He laughed. "The excise men do not frighten me. They could not find their own arses with a map."

Hannah tried not to react to the coarse language. Apparently her surprise must have shown itself on her face as his grin widened.

"So, this object cannot simply be brought over on a private ship?"

She shook her head. "Well, the problem is…" She felt heat surge into her cheeks. "No one will bring it over."

He scowled. "Why the devil not?"

She shrugged, feigning nonchalance. "It is large. Perhaps that's why."

He narrowed his eyes to two slits. "Will you tell me what this object is?"

"Will you take the job?"

"I hardly think that would be wise of me, until I know what it is."

Hannah huffed. She had little choice and he knew it. Besides, as much as they needed to keep their discovery quiet until it was safely in the museum in London, what would a common smuggler do with the knowledge?

"It is an Egyptian artifact. It is of vital historical importance."

She would not mention how it ended up in France or the troubles that her father had encountered. Many people might not care about the history behind such objects, but they would know well enough the profit to be made in such things.

"An artifact?" Both brows lifted.

"Yes."

"You wish to pay me to smuggle in an artifact that, for some unknown reason, no one else will."

"Yes."

He laughed. "Miss Hannah St. John, it has been a…pleasure indeed, but I find my drink is calling to me."

"You will not help me?"

Red shook his head. "Do you think me a fool? If lesser men have turned you down, you will not find me volunteering to help."

"But…"

"You have had a long day, as you said, Miss St. John.

Perhaps you should find a bed for the evening." He motioned to the serving girl. "Louisa will tell you if there are any spare rooms."

"I can pay you!"

He shook his head. "I don't need your money."

"So the infamous smuggler Red is scared."

He unfolded his arms and came close. "You forget who you are dealing with, Miss St. John. As you keep saying— extremely loudly—I am a smuggler. I break the law on a regular basis. Do not cross me. I will not say it so nicely next time."

Hannah searched his gaze while her heart trembled in her chest. Would he really harm her? She could not see it and yet, logically, she knew he was right. He was a smuggler, a man who thought himself above the law. What would prevent him from harming her if she did not leave him be?

Straightening, she tugged her pelisse tight around her and stood. "You have missed out on an excellent chance, Mr. Red. I would have paid well, and you could have had a piece of history under your command."

He smirked.

"Enjoy your drink," she said, her tone bitter.

Twisting away, she stormed out of the building and sucked in a gulp of salted air. The moon lingered behind new clouds, casting an intermittent glow over the sea below. She could hear the faint swish of waves. She would not go back in to get a room. Thankfully she had found a room in a cottage in the village not far from the inn. In truth, she had thought little about the practicalities of her journey, having been far too focused on her mission but she had been lucky to find accommodation with an elderly widow who hired out her room to young ladies travelling alone.

Damn that man.

"Insufferable. Vile. Horrible."

Where else would she find someone willing to help? Smugglers were hardly the easiest of men to track down. She had only known of Red through her father's letter as a colleague of his had taken part in some dealings with him when bringing over some expensive French wine that was no longer available because of the war.

Well, she would certainly not beg and nor did he deserve any part of her mission. Why, he should be honored to take part in such a momentous adventure. But, of course, what did a smuggler know of honor?

CHAPTER THREE

The wind from the previous day had vanished. Unfortunately, Red's fuzzy head had not. That damned Miss St. John had irritated him that much he'd proceeded to drink far more whiskey than intended simply to calm down. Even then, he'd found himself tossing and turning, thinking of her.

He lifted his hat to a passing couple, strolling along the promenade in their finery. He thought back to the rather frazzled-looking Miss St. John and silently cursed himself. The woman had shown utter disdain for him, so why should he give her one thought? As if he needed her money! Hell, he had more than enough to last him several lifetimes. It was clear she had little idea who he really was.

And that was the way he liked it.

He smiled genially as Mr. Longstead, the local fishmonger, paused to wish him good day. "Come to see your ship, my lord? I heard she got in last night."

Red glanced toward the harbor where the masts of the Endeavor could be seen amongst a few others. "Indeed."

"There was quite a squall last night. Lost a fishing boat

apparently. At least with a fine ship like yours there's no chance of that," the old man said.

"For that, I am grateful. Did you get a good catch in spite of the weather?"

Mr. Longstead paused to glance up at the sky, his white, bushy eyebrows lifting. "Not bad at all. The crews saw a couple of patrol ships out, though. Damned things don't half like to get in the way."

The man's skin was more creased than it should have been for his years, and the color of leather. Many years at sea before Mr. Longstead had settled to become a fishmonger were responsible for that. One of the many reasons Red preferred to stay on land. Let Drake worry about the squalls and the sunburned skin. His captain relished every part of being in charge of a ship.

"I suppose they must do their duty."

He snorted. "Their duty...they don't care about duty. They're greedy beggars, is all."

Red nodded slowly. Most of Cornwall, and he suspected much of the south coast of England, hated the excise men. Men like himself brought in cheap goods, some of which could not be bought in England since the war. As long as the smugglers treated the locals well, most supported them wholeheartedly. Of course, there were some awful brutes. Red had heard tales of towns being burnt to the ground because the smugglers were handed over. Thankfully there was no chance of that here. Either the townsfolk turned a blind eye, or they took advantage of the cheap goods.

Naturally, none of them were quite aware of his role in it. The Endeavor, he, and Drake were entirely innocent in the eyes of the townspeople. And that was the way it had to remain. He hated to think what drama and scandal there would be if their upstanding Earl of Redmere was discovered to be a smuggler. As much as they liked smugglers, they did not want their lord to be one.

"Well, I had better let you get on, my lord. I'm sure you have a busy day ahead."

"That I do. I shall send one of the lads down to check out your fresh catch later. I am sure the housekeeper will appreciate a decent bit of fish on the menu."

"Right you are. Good day." Mr. Longstead tipped his hat and moved on his way.

Red took a right along the edge of the harbor. Wooden bollards lined the stone edge, waiting for more ships, though Penshallow harbor rarely saw many big ships. His was the largest and therefore drew a fair amount of attention when in dock.

A few fishermen's cottages lined the harbor, packed close together, some painted white, while others were painted in shades of blue. The morning sun glinted off their tiny, dark-framed windows. Once again, he cursed the weather. Why could it have not been like this last night? If they'd have waited but one day, they could have brought in their haul with ease.

Although in the smuggling game, waiting at all was risky. Far better to get the goods ashore and distributed as quickly as possible. Thankfully that was what he had men like Nate for. His brother was the savviest businessman he'd ever met.

He paused outside the gangplank to the ship. A two-masted ship, the Endeavor was a well-equipped brig. Her sails were tucked safely away and her white and wooden hull gleamed. Nicholas Drake was about the best captain going, and Red was happy for him to be in charge of his ship.

"How goes it?" he shouted up.

Drake arrived in moments, stepped up to the gangplank and gestured for Red to come aboard.

"Captain," Red greeted.

"Red."

Though Drake had spent many years at sea before his leg injury, he showed no signs of wear and tear like the fishmonger. If it was not for his limp, his friend would look in fine health. With sandy hair, clear blue eyes, and more strength than most men, Drake was utterly unlike any seaman Red had ever met. When he had advertised for a captain for his ship, he had known instantly this was the man for him.

And he had never been proved wrong.

They moved down into the bowels of the ship and to the rear cabin. Drake offered him a drink, but Red shook his head. "I drank more than enough last night."

"Celebrating or drowning your sorrows?"

"Bit of both." Red sat, taking in the scent of sea and wood. Drake kept a fine ship, and his cabin was tidy and spotless. The only sign of inhabitance was his ship's log, resting on the desk, carefully filled with fictitious information.

"A hard night?"

Red nodded. "We did well though there were revenue men about. The weather made it damnably hard, however."

Drake poured himself a finger of brandy and sat opposite. "It was pretty choppy last night."

"Any problems?"

Drake smirked. "When has there ever been? The Endeavor dealt with it perfectly."

"She's a fine ship, with a fine captain."

Drake didn't acknowledge the compliment. He did not need to. His skills were known far and wide, and he'd led many a battle charge against France before he'd been struck by shrapnel in the leg.

"When shall we head out again?"

"I have a shipment of wine that will need to be collected from Spain in a few weeks—a legitimate shipment."

"Anything from France?"

Red shook his head. "Not for a while. This latest haul was big enough, it will take us a few weeks to move it on." He paused. "The men, they got off safely?"

Drake nodded. "They slipped in easily enough. The crew knows how to put on a show."

Red grinned. "You do a fine job of it."

He shrugged. "If we can help the war effort, that's good enough for me. A little profit on the side does not hurt, though."

Laughing, Red stood. "You'll get your share in two weeks. In the meantime, have the ship ready and enjoy yourself. If we happen to get any orders through, we'll need to make a quick trip across to France, but I have my doubts anything will arise."

Drake followed suit and stood. He led Red up onto the deck. "You ever think what we'll do once the war is over?" he asked, leaning against the mast.

"What do you mean?"

"We both know you're not in this for the money. The only ones who need the coin are me and Knight."

Red smirked. "You still need coin?"

The captain eyed his fingernails, a half-smile on his face. "Well, I would not mind more."

"You'll get plenty more, do not fear."

"But profit has never been your motivation. So once the smuggling stops being a cover to help the war effort, what then? Do we keep going? Or do we turn our attention to more legal means of profit?"

"Perhaps the war will never end."

Drake chuckled. "You know, I think, in spite of your bellyaching, you like the thrill."

Red lifted a shoulder. Sometimes he did. Sometimes he had to wonder if he had lost his senses, participating in such dangerous actions. There was always risk. The Crown's spy network might be aware of their actions, but they could never acknowledge as much—it would put every spy out there at risk and ruin any chance of using smuggling as a cover to get deep into France again.

"Well, whatever you decide, you will always have my service, Red. I'm indebted to you."

Red shook his head. He knew the captain felt his life was over after his injury. Unable to fight, he'd been lost and wound up in quite a bit of debt from gambling, even going as far as to lose his father's modest estate. When Red had met him, Drake had been a penniless, grizzled baron. The man in front of him was a far cry from that.

"You put your neck on the line for me every time you sail out—it is I who owe you."

A hand to Red's shoulder, Drake shook his head. "Let us call it even."

Red nodded. "I'll see you at the inn tonight?"

"Without a doubt."

"We'll need to get the cargo moved within the next few days. The excise men have been sniffing around."

"Whatever you need, Red."

"Excellent. I shall see you tonight."

Red made his way down the gangplank, mentally tallying up what they'd brought in last night and how they were going to disperse it. He had several regular customers and of course the townspeople would be wanting to purchase some of the goods. That was were Knight came in. The brooding hulk was the face of their operation, and it did not hurt that no one would dare cross him.

Opting to follow the harbor wall down to the town, he eyed the tiny cottages scattered across the hills. He had lived in Cornwall his whole life and avoided London at all costs. His father had never been a fan of it, and Red could never understand why anyone would want to travel such a distance just to be seen and spend time with the *ton*.

No, give him rolling hills, sandy beaches, quaint towns, and the slow Cornish pace any day.

He peered down the harbor, spotting the sails of the Bounty. He frowned. The Bounty was owned by Sir Michael Newport, a wealthy merchant who operated occasionally out of Penshallow. However, he had only made port here yesterday and they had conversed briefly then. His crew was to take a little shore leave before setting off again. So why were the sails raised?

He headed briskly over and paused to watch the men loading the ship. He shook his head and headed up the gangplank.

He froze.

"What the bloody hell are you doing here?"

Miss St. John spun on her heel, her head whipping around. "I could say the same about you."

"I asked first."

She jerked her chin up. Though she had looked a little frazzled

the previous night, the firelight had made her skin soft and her wispy curls touchable looking. He could not tell if the harsh sunlight made her more or less appealing. Her skin still appeared soft, with a hint of color from the fresh air on her cheeks. A few freckles danced across her nose, and her eyes were a warm nutty shade. Her hair was inky black and shiny. That nose she so boldly thrust up in the air was by no means the petite sort of thing that most women opted to have painted in their portraits, but it suited her stubborn chin and big eyes.

"Seeing as you would not help me, I have hired someone else. If you are now having regrets, it is too late."

"Regrets?" He chuckled. "The only one who should have regrets is you."

"Why? Because I did not get down on my knees and plead for the great smuggler Red to help me."

"No." He glanced around. "Because you have commissioned a stolen ship."

A man scurried up the gang plank and paused when he saw Red. He tried to turn around, but Red grabbed him by the scruff of the neck and dragged him backward.

"Fred Fletcher," Red said.

"My lord." The scruffy urchin of a man tried to bow, but Red kept him held upright by the scruff of his collar.

"My lord?" Miss St. John blurted. She shook her head. "Leave my captain be."

"Fred here is no captain."

"I certainly am," he protested.

Miss St. John folded her arms. "I demand you release him. We will be setting off shortly, and I must not be delayed."

Red blinked at her. "You are going with them?"

"Yes, they...well, they insisted."

Red shook his head. "Frederick, what the hell are you up to?"

"No-nothing, my lord. She's mistaken. We were just doing some work for Mr. Newport."

"And you decided it might be a good idea to commandeer his ship."

"Never!"

Looking at Miss St. John, Red lifted a brow. "Did this man offer to collect your artifact for you?"

"Yes! He simply wanted me to accompany them so I could be sure the artifact was handed over to them."

Red shook his head, dragged Fred down the gangplank and flung him to the floor. Miss St. John followed, squawking about his mistreatment of the man.

"Do not hurt him. I need him."

"This man, Miss St. John, is a liar and thief." He looked to the few men on deck. "And they are no better. They are well known in this area for getting into mischief."

"My lord," Fred protested.

"But this looks like more than a bit of mischief, does it not, Fred? Were you really planning on stealing a ship and taking Miss St. John goodness knows where? Perhaps you planned to ransom her. Fancied the pirate life, did you?"

Fred scrabbled to his feet, snatching up his hat and placing it on his head. "I planned no such thing."

Red stared him down and saw the man shrink into his boots a little. "Fred?"

The man turned to run away, but Red had him by the back of his coat once more and held him captive.

"We were only going to borrow the ship," he protested. "And the lady. She weren't going to come to no 'arm."

Miss St. John watched them both, wide-eyed.

"Did you give him coin?" Red asked.

She nodded. "Half now and half once we returned."

"Fred," Red warned.

"It's at the inn. We weren't going to do no 'arm, I swear."

"Did you really think you could steal a ship and no one would notice?"

The man's face colored an unpleasant purple hue. Red shook his head. Frederick Fletcher had been a petty criminal for some time, even serving jail time, but he had never done anything quite this bold. It seemed he had a taste for piracy or some other rash idea.

"Miss St. John," he thrust a finger at her, "come with me."

She opened her mouth to protest then nodded weakly.

He looked up at the ship. "Unless you lot want the local militia after you, I suggest you put down the sails and disembark with haste."

The men watching the show from the deck hastened down.

"As for you," he said to Fred, "we're going to visit the magistrate."

Fred groaned.

CHAPTER FOUR

Foolish.

No, Hannah felt more than foolish. Utterly idiotic. A complete imbecile. Was she not meant to be a smart woman? And yet she had let herself be taken in by petty criminals.

She pressed a hand to her ribcage. Goodness knows what they had intended to do with her.

Red gave her a sympathetic look which made her want to swipe it off his face. She withdrew her hand from her chest and straightened. Beaded reticule clutched close and now filled with her returned money, she sidled into the chair he had drawn out for her.

The private parlor in the Ship Inn was hardly much better than the rest of it, but at least it was peaceful. Hannah could scarce believe how many men were already propped up against the bar or back at the tables gambling away what little fortune they had. It was as though some of them had not even left for the night.

She perched carefully on the wooden chair, aware the wooden legs squeaked and wobbled a little when she did so.

It was not that she was an overly heavy woman—in fact she thought herself as quite average in most areas apart from intellect really—but the chairs had likely been in use for far longer than they should have been.

Gaze lowered, she eyed the scratched surface of the table, taking in the few barely legible names scrawled into it and scars from what must have been from knives. From poor table manners or from something else, she wondered. This was just the sort of place bar fights broke out. She lifted her gaze to Red as he seated himself opposite her.

Did he ever get in bar fights? And what was the lord thing about? Something to do with his position as a smuggler? She had heard of pirate lords in books. Perhaps it was something like that.

"Why Red?" she asked, the question bursting from her before she could prevent it.

His lips quirked, and he motioned for the woman from last night to serve them. "Have you eaten?" he asked Hannah.

"I..." She scowled. "A few hours ago."

He nodded. "A pie for both of us, please, Louisa. And two ales."

"I do not—"

"Today, you drink ale. You're pale."

"I was going to say, I do not need food." She turned a smile to Louisa. "An ale would be excellent, thank you."

Louisa grinned back and tucked her hands into her apron. "Pies and ales coming up."

Red waited until she had left before facing Hannah.

"You don't have red hair," Hannah mused. "Have you spilled lots of blood?"

"Gallons," he said dryly.

"No, that's not it. My father would not have suggested searching you out if you had."

"Your father sent you to me?"

She nodded. "You helped a friend of his."

"Ah." He leaned back and eyed her.

Unnerved by his study of her, she tried not to squirm in her seat and met his gaze head on. Her stomach did a twist that felt as though it would never untangle. His eyes were an intense blue, slightly at odds with his light brown hair. Some people would compare them to the ocean, but they would be doing them an injustice. The seas around England were a murky green color and nothing like the bold color of Red's eyes. His were more like the Caribbean Sea—not that she had ever seen it, but her father had described it perfectly.

"Tell me, why are you alone?"

She frowned. "My father is in France."

"And he lets you gallivant about alone."

"Of course. I have always been independent."

He shook his head. "There would be many who would be scandalized by such behavior."

She met his gaze head on and the knot in her stomach did another loop. "I am a gentleman's daughter," she insisted. "But I am hardly the owner of a fortune or a great reputation. My father trusts me to look after myself and stay out of harm's way, so I need no more permission than that."

"And yet, somehow you nearly got yourself kidnapped by would-be pirates."

"If you had accepted my offer that never would have happened."

His lips twisted. "So that was my fault, was it?"

"Absolutely. Had you not been so rude and listened to my offer, you would have accepted." She jabbed a finger his way. "You left me with no choice."

Louisa entered the room in a timely manner, bringing forth their ales and pies. Her stomach grumbled loudly in response to the fragrant smells of meat and gravy. Hannah saw Red press his lips firmly together to suppress a smile. She narrowed her gaze at him while she thanked Louisa.

Insufferable man.

"Pardon?"

Her eyes widened. Had she said that out loud? "It-it smells good."

His knowing gaze told her she had not done a good enough job of covering her slip. But then, why should she care? He had been nothing but rude and disagreeable since they had first met.

He took a long gulp of ale, and she watched his throat work. Never before had she found a man's Adam's apple to be interesting, but there was something wholly fascinating about the way it bobbed, making the stubble on his neck move with it.

He still had not shaved, she noted, although his hair was a little more tamed and respectable. He certainly did not look like a smuggler to her, but she supposed that was what made him such a good smuggler—no one would suspect him of criminal activities even if his manners were the coarsest she had ever witnessed.

Red wasted no time in digging into the pie. Her stomach renewed its protests at the sight of crumbling pastry and succulent meat. Apparently her stomach had seen fit to untangle itself. A poor tavern this might be, but the food looked wonderful.

"I'm not planning on poisoning you." He gestured to her untouched food.

"I know that," she snapped, drawing up her knife and fork.

He looked at the knife. "And I hope you are not planning on slicing my throat."

She glanced at how she was holding it, directed at him in

what could certainly be conceived as a threatening manner. Hannah lowered it. "I would never say never," she muttered.

He chuckled around a mouthful of meat, the sound genuine. She blinked at him. It was the first time she'd heard him laugh with genuine enjoyment, rather than in an attempt to make her feel foolish, and she could not help but like it.

Before she could make a further show of herself, she tucked into the food and took a sip of ale. Her attempt not to wrinkle her nose failed, and Red eyed her with a glint in his eye that told her he knew she had just been putting on a show of bravado and actually she never drank ale. The occasional sip of whiskey, yes, or even a brandy every now and then, but her father detested ale and she had always tended to follow his tastes on everything.

"So," he said, placing down his cutlery, "tell me more about this artifact."

"You are interested now?"

He sighed. "It seems I am. I can hardly let you go running off with more petty criminals, can I?"

"Can you not?"

"Apparently not," he grumbled.

She grinned. "So you do have some morals."

"Apparently so."

She took another sip of the ale, feeling the bitter tang fizz down her throat. It was not that bad, she supposed. At least it had the similar warming affect that whiskey did.

"The artifact is a large stone."

"A large stone?" Both his brows rose.

"It has inscriptions on." She leaned forward, unable to keep the grin from her face. "In different languages."

"Oh yes."

"Do you not see how exciting it is?"

"I can't say I do."

"This stone is thousands of years old. From Ancient Egypt."

"You did mention something about that. How did your father come about it?"

"My father has been an explorer since I was a little girl. He has been on many expeditions and is well respected in London intellectual circles. He has helped develop the collection of antiquities at the British Museum."

"How fascinating."

"Have you ever been to the museum, Mr. Red?"

"Just Red," he corrected. "And no. I had my head filled with enough history as a boy. I have done my best to avoid it ever since."

"Then you are missing out a great deal. My father always says, 'how can we move forward if we do not look back?'"

"Ah, well, there we differ. Looking back merely delays the going forward part."

She shook her head. "No, it does not. We must learn from our previous mistakes or else we will repeat them over and over."

He smirked. "I never make the same mistake twice."

"That I do not believe."

"Believe what you wish, Miss St. John, but you will not find me getting excited over a lump of rock." He drained his ale. "So he found this on one of his expeditions."

"No. This was in France. When Napoleon invaded Egypt, he took a lot of artifacts with him. He has been keeping them hidden. It is vitally important we take back as many as we can."

"To Egypt?"

"No, of course not. They must be brought here so we can study them."

"Do the Egyptians not have a problem with this?"

Hannah slid down into her seat a little. "Most of them try to sell their history. It must not end up in the wrong hands."

He leaned in toward her. "And who is to say your hands are the right ones?"

She paused and took a drink to cover her confusion. "Well, we cannot have Napoleon stealing all their history!"

"So you're the better thief?"

"The British Museum can protect the stone. They have the resources to study it. The Egyptians certainly do not, and Napoleon does not care for the history. It's all a display of power."

Red ran his finger around the rim of his ale, and they both watched the show for a moment.

Hannah took the chance to draw in a breath and cool her heated face. In truth, she had never considered what they did with the Egyptian artifacts could be wrong. In the recent years, it had become very popular to own pieces of Egypt's history and many items were bought and sold for large prices. Some grand houses even had mummies in them for goodness sake.

But that was not what she and her father wanted. No, they were not interested in simply having something to display. Their aim was to study these items, learn about them, create a knowledge base about the people of Egypt, and understand more thoroughly where they came from.

"So your father is in France rounding up various artifacts?"

She nodded. "Only the ones that are easily come by. He is five and fifty—hardly fit for spying. The stone had been left in storage in France, and he was able to bribe a soldier to gain access to it."

"And he has left you all alone for how long?"

"He has been gone several months." She frowned. "I am

not sure why you are so fixated on me being alone. Many women function quite well on their own."

"If I were your father, I would not leave you alone for a second. You are far too attractive to be left alone."

"I—"

"And far too much trouble."

Any warmth from the compliment vanished. "Look, Mr. Red, do you intend to help me or not? If not, please stop wasting my time. My father is in Le Havre, awaiting someone to take the stone."

Red's gaze lifted to hers and lingered on her face, dropping briefly to her lips. A faint half-smile played across his mouth. "I will help you. I'll be damned if you get yourself tangled up with criminals again."

The air left her body. "Thank you." Foolishly, tears danced in her eyes. She blinked them away. "Thank you."

He peered at her as if she was the oddest creature he had ever met.

Hannah could not bring herself to care what he thought. The artifact would be where it belonged soon enough, and she would have her father's pride. She hoped.

CHAPTER FIVE

"We're to do what?"

Red drew in a breath and faced his brother. Very slowly, he said, "We are to collect an artifact."

From over the table, Drake leaned forward. "But why?"

"Because the job pays generously," Red explained patiently.

"You said we weren't going out for a while." Knight leaned back in his chair and motioned to Louisa to bring him another ale.

The subtle din of the tavern covered their conversation well enough. The Ship had long been their base to discuss operations. Louisa, the owner, was well aware of their activities, and they repaid her kindness with cheap and free alcohol whenever they could. She had already covered their hides once or twice and would no doubt be called on to do so again one day.

As for the rest of the patrons, none cared enough about them to question four friends spending time together. Those who came to the Ship were here to drink, gamble, and often drown their sorrows. They cared little for the business of others.

Red rubbed a hand over his face. He knew he was going to have a hard time convincing them this was a worthwhile job. They had no information or men to slip into France, so why take the risk? But he had offered his help to Hannah, and he'd be damned if he'd go back on his word.

"Things change."

Nate shook his head and pushed his glasses back up his nose. "Since when?"

"Now, damn it."

Drake smirked. "You want to tell us the real reason we have to trek across the ocean for a bit of stone?"

Red swung his gaze from man to man. His clenched his jaw and huffed. "Very well. This woman came to me—"

His companions groaned. Knight shook his head and muttered *women* as though they were the very devil incarnated.

"She will pay us well," he continued.

"For some stone?" Nate asked.

"Yes. It is of historical importance." Christ, now he even sounded like Hannah, all prim and upright, yet excited about the prospect of more history. The way her eyes had lit up when she spoke of the stone had been the most enchanting— albeit a little baffling—thing he had ever seen. How could someone get so excited about history?

"Historical importance?" Knight's dry tone told Red the man was just as excited by the idea of fetching a stone as the rest of them.

He changed tact. "Napoleon stole many Egyptian artifacts during his invasion of the country. This woman's father is involved with recovering them."

"So we're stealing a stolen object that was stolen from

Egypt by Napoleon, and we're bringing it to England and not returning it to where it belongs?" Nate asked.

Red groaned inwardly. "Yes, that is about the measure of it."

His brother shrugged. "Sounds reasonable to me."

Drake laughed. "Oh yes, reasonable indeed." He leaned into Red. "Tell me about this woman."

"She is very pretty," Louisa said, bringing over a fresh ale for Knight. "Elegant, I would say. Red certainly liked her."

"I damn well did not," he muttered.

All the men chuckled.

Louisa tucked the serving tray under one arm and propped her hand on her hip. "I have never seen you have more than a five-minute conversation with a woman, let alone a full-blown argument."

"*You* should not have been listening," he scolded.

"It could hardly be helped. You were not the quietest."

"And it was not an argument. We were merely debating."

She shook her head. "Well, if you ask me, you were thoroughly enjoying your debate."

"No one asked you," he grumbled.

Louisa did a poor job of smothering a giggle. "Can I get you gentlemen anything else?"

Knight grunted. "Keep them coming."

She ran her gaze over the hulk and lifted her brows. "As you will." She turned to Red's brother. "Say, Nate, the stable hand says we have your pet sheep in the barn. I didn't think you the sort to have a fondness for livestock."

"I did not." Nate sighed. "*I do not.*"

Louisa's brows rose.

"The sheep adopted him," Drake explained.

"Adopted him?"

"The blasted animal won't leave me be. I tried to take it back to where I found it, but it seems it's become split from its flock. So, well—" Nate's face reddened "—she's mine now I guess."

Louisa barely smothered a smile and even Red needed to bite down on his tongue. The sheep had been following Nate everywhere and had now taken up residence in the barn near their home. It had been a fight to keep the damn animal from trying to follow Nate into the house. He could just imagine his mother rising from the grave to scold them for letting an animal traipse across the Persian carpets.

"Does she have a name?" the innkeeper asked.

Nate glared at her. "Of course she damn well does not."

"Come now, Nate." Drake grinned. "Your pet must have a name."

"How about Fluffy?" Louisa suggested.

"Or Snowy," Red put in.

His brother's glare darkened.

"What about Cloudy?" Red said, barely smothering a laugh.

"Franklin," Knight said gruffly.

They all turned to the giant in the corner. "Franklin?" Louisa queried. "Franklin is a terrible name for a sheep."

He shrugged. "I had a cat called Franklin."

Silence fell like a hammer across the table. If the other people in the room were anything like Red, they were firstly baffled by the idea of Knight ever owning an animal. It was hard to picture those huge hands stroking across a cat's head or those big fingers tickling a fluffy tummy. And secondly, this was about the most personal admission they had ever heard from Knight. Red trusted the man with his life, but he knew very little about Lewis Knight, save that he fought in France for some time before returning to England and running into some trouble with the law.

Louisa cleared her throat. "Well, I shall ensure Fluffy is well looked after. I probably have some leftovers she'll enjoy."

"She's not called Fluffy," Nate protested.

Knight huffed. "I still like Franklin."

Nate lifted a hand. "Can we not get back to the fact that Red has signed us up for some adventure all in the name of a woman?"

Drake turned his gaze to Red. "Oh yes, I think we should. We need all the important details. Is she attractive?"

Red curled a hand around his glass of ale. "I do not see what that matters."

"Very well, it's not that important anyway." Drake's grin turned lascivious. "Does she have big tits?"

Groaning, Red clenched down on his jaw until it hurt. If this woman had him close to fighting his friends, Lord knows what other chaos she could cause.

CHAPTER SIX

A gust of wind threatened to blow off her bonnet. Hannah put a hand to it and continued her pacing.

She had been walking along the harbor since early morning. A storm had come in off the sea overnight, and puddles pooled between the cobbles. She lifted her skirts to avoid getting too wet as she walked briskly past the wooden bollards and eyed the few fishing vessels lined up alongside.

Her skirts were less of a concern than the Endeavor, however. What if it had become caught in the storm? What if it had sunk with the stone on board? What if they had not caught up with her father or he had moved elsewhere, giving up on hope of her sending someone to collect it?

She made her way to the long stone jetty that signaled the entrance to the harbor. From here, she had a fine view of the sea. The line of grey ocean revealed a depressingly empty sight. No sails could be seen. She paused by the lighthouse that sat at the end of the pier and rested against the stone.

Hannah covered a yawn. She had hardly slept the previous night, knowing the stone would be on its way to England and if all went well, the ship would be back today.

Excitement and anxiety bubbled in her stomach. Red might not understand the importance of such a find, but this artifact was entirely unique and unlike anything else found in Egypt. They would be able to learn so much from it.

"How long have you been here?"

She whirled and her hem caught under her heel. Red put out a hand to steady her, and she instinctively reached for it.

"Careful now, I have little intention of getting wet today."

"Why would you?"

"If you fall in, I'd have to rescue you."

She peered at him and finally glanced at their hands which were still joined. Withdrawing her hand quickly, she tried to force away the memory of his touch which had left an odd warm sensation on her skin, even through her gloves. She ran her gaze over his clothing. From his hessians to his tail coat, he was every inch the gentleman. She cocked her head.

"What is it?"

"I do not think you would rescue me."

"You have me pegged as quite the rapscallion, do you not?"

"You are a smuggler, are you not?"

He leaned in. "You must stop using that word, Miss St. John. You do seem to forget that being a smuggler is not the most honest means of making a living. I would rather most people remained in ignorance as to my...occupation."

She laughed. "I am not sure many would be bold enough to call it an occupation."

"Oh, and what would you call it?"

His closeness addled her wits. It left her usually clear and sensible mind fuzzy. Hannah could not say why but the fresh, soapy scent of him that had suddenly curled itself about her like a vine might have had something to do with it.

"A criminal activity," she said, trying to keep her voice strong.

"Do not forget, Miss St. John, that you are now associated with criminals." He eased back and straightened. "I should be careful what accusations you throw about."

"I throw nothing about. I merely speak the truth. Accusation implies that there might not be truth behind it."

He grinned as his gaze landed on something behind her. "Ah, that will be them." He pointed to the merest dot on the horizon.

She narrowed her gaze. Sure enough the dots turned into the hint of a sail and eventually a ship.

"I am glad they made it through the storm," she murmured.

"Drake is the finest captain at sea. He has faced worse than a small squall."

"Some of the fishermen said it was one of the worst they'd seen in several years."

Red shook his head. "Drake's come up against worse."

"Where exactly did you come across him? How does one persuade someone to step onto a path of criminal behavior?"

He twisted to view her. Goodness, she wished he did not have such wide shoulders or penetrating eyes. They burrowed into her, ensuring she was left a little breathless. He had to be the most—she wanted to say intimidating man —but that was not it.

The most intense man she had ever met.

"One persuades a man down such a path with ease when one offers him the right things."

"Coin, I suppose."

"Something like that." He peered at her down his nose. "Miss St. John, you are very intent on insulting me at every turn, are you not? Considering I have aided you and that the stone is not yet in your hands, I do not think it remiss of me to expect a little more politeness."

Hannah dropped her gaze to the stone surface of the pier. She eyed the dips in it, worn from years of sea spray and footsteps. She was never normally so rude...and he was right, she was being rude. There was something about him that immediately drew up her defenses. Whenever she saw him, she felt like a castle under siege. She had to draw up the bridge and prepare the boiling oil.

"I—"

"Of course, I could just drop the damned stone over the side of the ship then you would learn your lesson."

A furious sound escaped her. To think she was about to apologize to the man. Why, he did not deserve a moment of her politeness.

"You, sir, are a scoundrel."

"Of the highest measure," he said smugly.

Blowing out an exasperated breath, she focused her attention on the nearing ship.

"Let us make our way down the harbor," he said, offering her his arm.

He knew she would ignore it and ignore it she did. His chuckle as she marched ahead had her spine straightening a little bit more. If she became any more rigid, she would snap in two. What was it about this man that did this to her?

As the ship approached them, Hannah became aware of the tattered state of the sails. It seemed the ship had gone through the storm and barely survived. In her ears, her heart drummed a heavy beat. She had to keep herself from jumping from foot to foot. Any moment now, she would be able to see the stone, to touch it. Something that was thousands of years old. She could not help herself—she grinned widely.

Hannah caught Red's bemused look but ignored it. He would not ruin this moment for her.

The men tied up the ship and set out the gangplank. It took far too long in her opinion. She twined her hands together and rose onto tiptoes for sign of the stone. Several men disembarked and approached them both.

"What the devil is wrong with you?" Red asked one of them—a large man that she recalled seeing at the inn. He was nearly doubled over, his skin pasty, with his arm around another man.

"He's sick," said the man holding the giant up. He pushed his glasses up his nose. His hair color was similar to Red's and they were close in build with wide shoulders and a dip in his jaw.

The third man came forward. "Hell of a journey. Never had one like it. Knight got sick as soon as we left Le Havre. We were hit by a severe squall last night. There's damage to the rigging and the sails. It's going to take some repairs."

Red cursed under his breath. "I should never have sent you lot over. You'd have done better with a more experienced crew."

The man, who she assumed was Captain Drake, shook his head. "These two made a good replacement for the crew that were on leave and it should have been an easy trip, but I tell you, Red, it was a memorable one. What with Knight being sick everywhere and the waves we faced..." He shook his head. "The sooner that stone is off my ship, the better."

"Is it here?" she asked eagerly.

All heads whipped around to face her.

"Is this her?" the Captain asked.

Red nodded. "Gentlemen, this is Miss St. John, our temporary employer." He motioned to the ship. "Let us get that damned stone off, and we can get this over with."

Drake signaled to two men on board, and they began

down the gangplank with the stone. It was wrapped in fabric so she could see nothing of it yet, and she would not unwrap it until she was safely ensconced in a private room some-where. The stone would need careful handling and studying. She certainly was not prepared to awe over it in front of these men.

"You had better get Knight home," Red said to the man propping him up.

The man nodded. "I'll see you at Whitechapel?"

"I'll be home shortly," Red agreed.

Hannah could not keep her gaze off the bundle of fabric. The two men laid it down on the harbor side.

She could not prevent herself from shouting, "Careful," as they put it down none too gently.

"Miss St. John, my men have been through hell and back for that stone," the Captain declared. "They have little inten-tion of breaking it. I do hope it's worth it."

"Oh it is, Captain, it really is."

Drake turned his attention back to Red. "I'll have to arrange repairs if we're to set sail again in a few weeks. It will be costly."

Red waved a hand. "Do what you must."

Running his gaze over Hannah, she tried not to squirm under his perusal. The Captain was a handsome man in spite of his limp and several small scars on his forehead. No doubt he was used to women swooning at his feet. However, she was utterly unused to men eyeing her figure so closely.

"Oh, I have a letter from your father." The Captain drew out some paper from his breast pocket.

She took it eagerly and popped it open.

"Thank you, Captain."

"You were right," he said to Red with a twinkle in his eye and made a cupping gesture with his hands. "Good day to you, Miss St. John. I hope you enjoy your stone and it brings you better luck than it did me."

She frowned while the Captain made his way back onto the ship. "Whatever did he mean?"

Red shook his head and chuckled. "You do not want to know, Miss St. John."

She cast her gaze over her father's scrawled letter. It was much as his communications usually were—vague, hurried, and full of excitement over history.

"He has tracked down another few artifacts. He will be several more months it seems." He eyed her until she was forced to ask, "What is it?"

"And you will be well, being on your own for several more months?"

"Of course." She urged a smile across her face. "I am used to it. Father has travelled since I was a child. Sometimes I went with him, but obviously he would not let me go to a war zone."

Shrugging, he offered out his hand. "Well, Miss St. John, I would say it has been a pleasure, but it seems you have cost me a fair bit in repairs and well..."

"I have yet to pay you the rest yet, Mr. Red. It will more than cover your expenses."

"Far be it for me to be rude and request payment, but I certainly would not complain. Shall we complete our business here or at your lodgings?"

"Complete our business? I still need to get the stone to London."

"And you will go with my blessings. The men seem to think it is cursed. The sooner it is gone from our town, the better."

Hannah huffed. That was exactly the reason no Frenchman would help. This idea of a curse was beyond foolish. "I do not want your blessings— I want your help."

He stilled. "Pardon?"

"To get to London." She gestured to the stone. "How am I to move such a thing to London? The deal was you would help me get it there. Half before you left, half when the stone was safely in the museum."

He shook his head vigorously. "No, Miss St. John, you never said that at all."

"I said half when it is done."

"Done, yes. As in across the ocean. Away from France. In your hands. Not carted all the way to London. Frankly you and your stone have caused me more trouble that its worth and I have little intention of spending more time with either of you."

CHAPTER SEVEN

Red paused before knocking on the cottage door. Damn suspicious fools. It was only a stone.

Mrs. Bell answered and dropped into a deep curtsey. "My lord, what brings you here?"

He smiled through his tension at the old lady who was burrowed deep in a knitted shawl. "I have come to call for your guest Miss St. John."

"Indeed." A twinkle behind her glasses made him grit his teeth. He had certainly not come here to enjoy Miss St. John's company. Hell, he'd rather be having his fingernails pulled out one by one than doing what he had to do, but no one would settle until the stone was gone. Even Knight, the bravest man he knew, was on edge after his bout of sickness.

"Will you come into the parlor? I shall call up to her."

"Thank you." Red removed his hat and ducked under the low beam of the fisherman's cottage.

The tiny parlor barely seemed to fit him, but he somehow squeezed onto a small chair that was carefully twisted to face the fire. He assumed the chair opposite was Mrs. Bell's as it was stuffed with cushions, and some needlework rested on the arm. The amber glow of the fire was the only light in the room and the one square window let in little dull sunlight. Wood crackled in the fire, giving off a pleasant smoke scent.

Miss St. John immediately drew his attention when she stepped into the room. Mrs. Bell offered to make tea, but they both refused. Leaving the door ajar, the old woman let them be.

"What are you doing here?"

For an instant, he forgot. Only one day had passed since he thought he'd seen the last of Miss St. John, and he had almost forgotten how wide and attractive her eyes were. The fire made her glossy hair shine, and it contrasted with her pale skin. He could not help but smile at the sight of those freckles, playing their merry way across her nose.

"Well?" she demanded, still not sitting.

"Have you found someone to move your stone?"

She shook her head.

"Then," he sighed, "I am here to offer my services."

"You will help me get the stone to London?"

"Yes."

"Why?"

There was something in her dipped brows and inquisitive gaze that had him confessing. "The men think the stone is cursed."

She blinked several times before laughing. "Cursed?"

"Yes. They attribute the storm and Knight's illness and a few other things to it."

He would not mention their close run in with a navy ship or the fact that Louisa's inn had been searched while the Endeavor had been gone. It was some rotten luck, though Red was not nearly as suspicious as Drake who, as a seaman was in inherently superstitious, and it had apparently rubbed off on the others.

"That's ridiculous."

"Do you want my help?"

She nodded frantically. "I must get it to London for study as soon as possible. There's a mail coach that leaves from Falmouth tonight. Can you be ready by then?"

"We can do better than that, Miss St. John. Can you be ready within the hour?"

"Of course."

"My coach is waiting outside."

She peered out of the window. He did not look too, but he knew what she'd see. His private coach, led by four horses. Black, shiny and painted with his family crest. His driver and footmen waiting patiently.

Miss St. John rotated slowly back to him, her mouth ajar. "That—" she pointed a finger out of the window "—is yours?"

"Yes." He tried to prevent a smug smile from slipping across his face.

"How can a smuggler afford that?"

"Do you really expect me to tell you?"

"I'm not sure I want to know." She peered out of the window once more and shook her head. "I shall gather my belongings, and we can set off presently."

By all accounts, Miss St. John was an efficient woman. She took a mere half an hour to have her trunks packed. Red ordered the footmen to load them onto the carriage along with the stone which Miss St. John insisted would have to remain with them in the coach.

Once the stone was loaded in, they bid Mrs. Bell farewell and set off. "We can stop at a coaching inn in Truro for the night."

She nodded and settled herself against the plush seat. Her eyes darted here and there, taking in the lavishness of his vehicle. As they set off, her gaze finally landed on him.

"You are not just a smuggler, are you?"

"No."

"Your crest...you are nobility, are you not?"

"Yes."

"How could you not tell me?"

"You did not ask."

She huffed. "I did but then I...I forgot."

"And I had no reason to remind you."

"Will you tell me who you are?"

He peered at his nails and let her sit in silence for a moment with only the horse hooves and the rattling coach for company. After some time, he decided to put her out of her misery.

"I am the eighth Guy Kingsley, Earl of Redmere."

"Oh, that is why they call you Red."

"Indeed."

"But why?"

"Why what?"

"Why smuggle? Why the secrecy? Why not tell me?"

"Firstly, because I want to. Secondly, because in case you had not noticed, smuggling is illegal. And thirdly, because you are not the quietest of women."

"So you do not trust me?"

"I do not trust your rather loud voice. That is entirely different to not trusting you," he pointed out.

She peered at him through the shadows of the carriage. "That is not logical."

Red leaned back and folded his arms. "Logic is overrated."

Miss St. John clutched her reticule as though his words might leap out an attack her. "Logic is imperative. Without it we could not function as a society. Imagine if everyone behaved illogically, it would be a disaster."

"There is a difference between acting logically and occasionally taking chances and ignoring logic."

An exasperated sound left her. "You are impossible. I'm not arguing with you."

"Excellent. I could do with some peace and quiet."

She snapped her attention to the view outside the window.

The oddest part of him had hoped she might continue. There was something intriguing about the fire in her eyes and the vehemence in her voice. The only other woman who spoke to him in a manner anything like the way Miss St. John did was Louisa and, frankly, she had every right to do so. They used her inn as a base and had been helped by her many times. But even then, she did not address him quite like Miss St. John did. Christ, he could not imagine any of the local gentry talking to him so. Most of the women were too busy angling for a proposal to think about arguing with him.

He eyed her profile. Her lips were still a little pursed and rather too appealing. Several glossy curls touched her cheeks, softening the look. She would make a perfect silhouette he decided. Her strong nose and chin were practically designed for silhouette painters.

She glanced at him sideways, and he turned his gaze toward the scenery. It had been a while since he had travelled this way. They were following the coastal path that linked the many seaside towns. In spite of intermittent clouds, he could still appreciate the rugged scenery of Cornwall. Much of it was distinguished by hills that led down to the various estuaries. Around them, villages had grown, the cottages spilling up the hills. Most of them made their living through fishing—as did many of the people in his own town.

As promised, Miss St. John did not argue with him, nor did she utter another word as they made their way to Truro. They stopped briefly to water the horses and give them a rest and, even then, she ignored him, opting to remain in the carriage with her precious piece of stone. When he clambered back in, he could not help but be jealous of the way she stroked it. Her delicate fingers ran over the carvings in it as though she were stroking a lover.

Red scowled at himself. Why he should reflect on Miss St. John and lovers in the same thought, he did not know. There was no chance the woman had ever taken a lover. Why, she was only, what—two and twenty at most—and with a spine as rigid as hers, there was no chance she had let a man under her stays.

And yet, he could not shake the thought that those fingers, so very perfect for touching and stroking, were entirely wasted on a piece of stone.

"Tell me about it," he said, weary of the silence.

She lifted her gaze to his as though she had almost forgotten he was there. "You really want to know?"

He nodded. Why not? He might as well learn something from this trip.

"The stone was found by the French when they were restoring a fort some years ago. Scholars often accompanied them much like my father. It was clear the stone was important, because it is written in two different languages." She pointed to one. "Greek, which we can read, and hieroglyphs, which we cannot."

He peered at the images on the stone. "They look like little drawings."

"Yes. You will have seen them on many Egyptian things, no doubt."

"I have a few replicas with similar looking sketches on them."

"We have never been able to decipher them, in spite of many people trying. There has never been anything with which to compare it to but this stone—" she released a long breath, her eyes wild with excitement "—this stone provides what we believe is a translation. If studied properly, we could unlock the key to understanding hieroglyphs. Our knowledge of the ancient Egyptians would vastly increase."

"You really love history, do you not?"

"I do."

Her excitable smile reminded him of a child who had just been given sweetmeats. It was ridiculously charming. It made him want to leap forward and press a firm kiss to her lips, simply to try to absorb some of her charm.

"Your father encouraged that love?"

She nodded. "My mother died nearly nineteen years ago when I was a baby."

Christ, that made her twenty. A grown woman by all accounts but eleven years his junior and too young to his mind to be gallivanting about the country, rescuing stones and associating with criminals.

"My father has a small estate, one that allows us to live modestly." She smiled. "Nothing like you are used to I imagine. But it meant he was always able to continue his studies. With my mother gone, he took it upon himself to teach me all he knew. My earliest memory is of being in his study, holding a canopic jar."

"A canopic jar?"

"A jar that the Egyptians used to store the internal organs of a deceased person in."

"What a lovely memory," he said dryly.

She did not seem to notice his sarcasm and continued, "My father was not the most practical of men, but he always loved to share his knowledge. I was in the care of a governess for much of the time, but I had little use for her. She could not teach me nearly as much as he could. When he came back from his travels, he would tell me all about what he had learned." She sighed. "Those were my favorite times."

"Did you not miss him?" There was something about

picturing a tiny Miss St. John anxiously awaiting the return of her father that made his gut ache.

"Naturally, but I understood why he had to be away. What could be more important than history?"

His own daughter, Red muttered inwardly.

Miss St. John carefully wrapped up the artifact as though it were a newborn baby. He could not help but admire her passion for the past. He had always tended to look to the future. As an heir, what else could one do? He had spent his whole childhood being groomed to take on the role of earl. Once it had happened, his sights had been set on improving the living of his tenants and perhaps taking a wife.

That had all changed when his brother had been refused a commission in the army though. It had been all he had ever wanted, but Nate's eyesight was not up to it. It did not matter that he could probably fight better than half of the officers already enlisted.

"You must miss your father," she said quietly, perhaps assuming his silence was for some other reason.

"It has been ten years now. He was a good man. My mother also passed away when I was young when my brother Nate was born. My father did a fine job of raising us alone."

"It seems we're are not so very different."

Except his father had not run off in search of history. He had remained at home, doing his best to instill values into them both. When he had passed away when Red was only one and twenty, it had been a great blow to them both. Red was determined to be the best man he could be in his honor and ensure Nate was afforded every opportunity as his father would have wanted.

Not that his brother would be impressed with him effectively mothering him, but Nate did not need to know that was what Red was doing.

They fell into silence. Whether Hannah was contemplating her own childhood or dreaming of the stone, he did not know, but he could not help think of his motherless childhood and compare it to hers.

At some point, Red dozed off. He knew this because he awoke with a start, his mouth dry and feeling disorientated.

"Red," someone hissed.

He grumbled and swung his gaze to the annoyance.

"Red," she said again.

His gaze landed on Miss St. John. God, she was pretty.

A blush filled her cheeks. "That is very nice of you to say, but now is not really the time for compliments."

He scowled. Had he said that aloud?

"What is going on?" he asked, his voice raw.

"We are stuck. The footmen are trying to push us out."

"Damn." He popped open the window and leaned out.

Sure enough they were buried deep in thick, black mud. It should not have been a surprise. The roads were notoriously bad out of Cornwall, which was why most people tended to avoid travelling out if at all possible. It was certainly a good excuse for him to avoid London at all costs. With the storms and inclement weather, he should have guessed his heavy coach would never make it through.

Unbuttoning his jacket, he shucked it off and unhooked his cufflinks before stowing them in his jacket pocket.

Miss St. John studied him. "What are you doing?"

"Getting out and pushing by the looks of it."

CHAPTER EIGHT

I t was ridiculous to feel anyway excited by the sight of Red trying to push the coach out of the mud. Ridiculous.

And yet Hannah's heart beat rapidly and this well of anticipation kept bursting at random intervals into her stomach. With his sleeves rolled up, mud covering his breeches and hessians and a few splatters on his shirt, he was quite the sight. Sweat trickled down his face, and his hair curled at the collar. His cravat was long gone.

She held her reticule tight against her chest. Their luggage sat at the side of the road and the stone lay carefully atop it. The four men had been trying to get the coach out for over an hour but to no avail. Meanwhile Hannah had to sit on a nearby rock and watch. Goodness, even she was beginning to perspire, and it certainly had nothing to with the weather. A brisk wind swirled about the hills, ruffling the lace of her bonnet. She tightened the ribbon about her neck to ensure it did not blow away.

Red stopped, placed his hands on hips and took a breath. She saw him shake his head and mutter something to the driver. He strode over to her, taking great big steps through the thick mud. He had been forced to lift her across the mud, and it had to be the strangest experience she had ever had. The only man to touch her so familiarly was her father. No other man had held her so, to be sure. Holding onto his arms and feeling the strength and heat of his skin through his shirt would linger with her for an eternity, she suspected.

"It's no good," he said, dabbing his forehead with his shirt sleeve.

Her mouth was dry. So dry. Like a desert. Or…or something even drier. There simply had to be something. Whatever it was, it made her tongue feel thick and useless. She merely offered some expression that hopefully portrayed a question—what would they do next?

"We can return on the horses."

She shook her head.

"I thought you might say that."

She did not bother to point out that she had said nothing so far. Instead she coughed to remove the awkward silence from her throat. "If we return, who knows when we shall be able to travel again. I do not think the weather will improve anytime soon."

He nodded. "These roads will take some time to dry out." He motioned along the dirt track. "We are not far from an inn, according to my driver. We shall have to abandon the coach and the horses will need to be returned—we'll have no use for them once we find alternative transport."

"If it is not far, that sounds the best option."

"We have little other choice. There is no sense in trying to bring other carriages through here. I doubt even my chaise can make it through this."

He glanced over his shoulder at the young, wiry footman who had been making an admirable attempt at trying to push the coach out of the mire. He looked the most exhausted out of all of them.

"Will you be needing me to carry your luggage, my lord?"

Red shook his head. "Mr. Greaves could do with some help returning the horses. There is no sense in you coming along. Get back home and you can help when they send up more men and horses to drag the vehicle out."

The young lad nodded.

Hannah eyed their luggage. "We cannot carry it all alone."

"That lad is about to drop. I have little intention of carrying an exhausted footman to the next inn. Besides, Mr. Greaves will need help taking the four horses back. They are about as exhausted as Harry."

She sighed. "As long as we get to London eventually."

"It is either this or we wait for the weather to clear at Whitechapel Hall."

"Your home, I presume?"

"Yes."

It was easier now, to picture him in a grand stately home, in spite of the mud slicked up his boots and splattered across him. His disheveled state might be far from gentlemanly, but it somehow worked for him. He at least made a little more sense to her. Why an earl would play pirate, she did not know, but his arrogance and well-groomed, crisp appearance were at least logical.

"I can leave the trunk. Perhaps you can have the men take it back and send it on once the roads are dry."

"I can do that."

"That only leaves my bag and the stone, though I shall have to transfer another dress or two to last me the journey."

"If I take only my satchel, we can carry it all easily between us."

Yes, she thought, eyeing those muscled arms that bulged against the seams of his shirt. He would have no trouble carrying the stone. A sigh escaped her.

"Never fear, Miss St. John, I shall protect you."

Protect her? Oh Lord. A swirl of sensation swept through her like gale, settling low into her stomach and threading through her legs. If she did not focus very carefully on keeping her knees locked, she might collapse all together. Red had not understood the reason for her sigh but had managed to make it twenty times worse. It was all entirely ridiculous. She could not fathom it, but for some reason, his offer of protection plucked at some delightful invisible string inside of her.

Ha. She did not even need protection. Hannah had travelled all the way to Cornwall alone safely. Simply because he had strong arms and a wide chest did not mean he could protect her any better than she could. Why, he might even attract trouble. She would have to be on her guard.

For trouble...and for him. Red could slip easily under her defenses, she feared.

Red arranged to have the luggage stowed in the carriage. They simply had to hope no one would come along and take it. The roads were so bad, she thought it unlikely. Once the men were sent on their way, she and Red began their journey west, following the grassy ledge at the side of the boggy road.

Hannah walked behind Red, who had opted to leave off his great coat, apparently still warm from his exertions. His shirt was untucked but through the linen she could see the outline of his rear. She had to admit, she had never eyed a man's bottom before. And there was good reason why. It meant she stumbled several times and nearly landed in the mud.

Wind whirled around her, picking up speed. She clutched her traveling bag to her as the gust breezed around her ankles and underneath her pelisse.

"Should not be far now," Red called.

She nodded but the hills were barren for as far as they could see. The coastline curved around, rising up sharply.

Her shoulders were beginning to ache and she could only imagine how Red felt, although he continued on as though the stone and his heavy bag were as light as a feather pillow.

Clouds gathered as they reached the headland. Red paused and squinted into the distance. "Ah, see there."

Air escaped her chest. "Yes, yes I do!"

A lone, white building sat humbly in the distance. It would only take them another half an hour to reach. Thank goodness.

The wind continued to buffet them. So much so that Hannah had to lean forward to walk into it. Where they were, exposed on the hills, there was no shelter or release from it. It was like wading through the sea and just as tiring. She paused to set down her bag on a rock briefly and roll her arms.

"Not far now," Red assured her, following suit and setting down the stone and his bag.

She eyed the building. Indeed, they were closer, but not close enough.

As another blast struck them, her hat loosened and lifted off her head. The grips ripped out of her hair and even though she scrabbled to grab it, it was gone in a trice. She twisted to watch it lift higher then swoop down over the cliff edge.

"Blast."

"Long gone now, I fear," Red said.

She nodded. "Never mind. It was not even my favorite."

He gave a good stretch, and Hannah found herself tracing the length of his body with her gaze. Her father had always said the best way to learn about something she did not understand was to study it closely. She was also certain he was not referring to men. Yet she could not help herself.

Men had always baffled her, however. She only under-stood her father and that was likely because they had spent twenty years together. A few local men had paid her a little attention, but she had hardly understood how to converse with them and they did not seem at all pleased with her passion for history. It seemed to her, they all wanted a woman who would be interested in them—and only them. Unfortunately, none could hold her attention long.

Red could, though. She was still staring. A great deal. Too much, really. Particularly because he was now looking at her in an odd manner.

"What is it?"

She shook her head to clear it. "Nothing. Let us get moving before this wind blows me off the cliff."

He chuckled. "Yes, we cannot let that happen. I don't much fancy diving off a cliff to rescue you."

There he went again, playing her charming protector. She would almost rather he was being rude and arrogant. At least she knew how to deal with that.

The clouds above darkened further while they progressed toward the inn. Hannah narrowed her gaze at them. *Do not rain, do not rain.*

It appeared she had no more command over the clouds than she did the muddy roads. The first big, fat drop struck her nose and tickled down her face. She swiped it aside, but the clouds split in an angry manner, pouring their vengeance upon them. Whatever they had done to deserve it, she could not say.

Red motioned for her to hurry, but neither of them could move any quicker, encumbered with their luggage and the stone. Rain drops invaded under her pelisse and soaked her hair to a floppy mess. Dips in the road filled instantly, and it was near impossible to avoid them. Even her stockings could not avoid getting soaked. By the time they had approached the inn, she was certain there was no part of her that remained dry.

Red paused in front of the door and shoved his soaking hair back from his face. She heard him curse under his breath so she finally peered at the building through the sheeting rain. This was no comforting traveler's inn. At least not anymore. Once upon a time perhaps the windows had been lit with a reassuring glow or the door had been freshly painted and the windows had not been broken in places.

That time was no more, however.

"Oh no."

"It must have closed," Red said to her, his words almost drowned out by the heavy pattering and the occasional whoop of wind across them. "Let us look inside. We cannot stay out here."

He twisted the knob and pushed open the door. Hannah's insides gave a twist with it. She was hardly superstitious, nor did she believe in ghosts or anything of the like. There was always a logical explanation for these things to her mind. However, the dank, dark interior of the empty inn made her shudder. She could well have put that down to her rain-soaked garments, but there was nothing pleasant about stepping into an abandoned building.

The door blew shut behind her, and she screamed.

Red whirled and gave her a look that told her she had nearly forced him to keel over.

"Sorry."

He grimaced and eyed the interior. "It is hardly what we were hoping for but it will have to do for now. We can't continue on in that weather."

Hannah nodded, clutching her bag to her. They were in the main room. The bar remained, thick with dust. A few chairs and tables were scattered about haphazardly. One or two tankards sat upon the fireplace as if waiting for their owners to come and have a drink from them. The air smelled stale, and there was a slight shuffling sound coming from above them. Something had likely taken this battered old inn as its home.

Another shudder wracked her.

"You're frozen," he stated.

As if on cue, her teeth started to chatter. She nodded, unwilling to admit the shudder was caused more by the barren and ghostly state of the building.

"You should change. Slip into the other room and change there. I suspect I can rustle up enough wood for a fire from this furniture, and I have my tinder and flint with me." He picked up an old stump of a candle. "There's enough of a wick here for us to find our way around for a moment. Hopefully it's not damp."

She glanced at the door to which he had motioned. The slowly building lump in her throat grew. She shook her head.

He lit the candle after a few tries and set it into a dusty old stand. "Hannah?"

"I-I'm not going in there."

He peered at her, one brow raised. Damn him. With his hair damp, his jacket now removed and his shirt almost stuck to his skin, he looked more handsome and devilish than ever. Devilish should not have been an appealing thing to be, and yet it was.

And, of course, she likely looked as though she had been pulled through a ringer. She could feel her curls dropping down her neck. Why was rain so flattering to men and so utterly ruining to women?

"You need to get out of those clothes, Hannah. If you're worried for your safety, let me assure you, I have no intention of stealing a look or doing anything untoward."

She tried to clamp her jaw shut to prevent the chattering of her teeth and failed. "I-I did not assume you would."

His lips quirked. "How trusting of you."

"I am sure a man like you has no need for sneaking looks

at vulnerable women. You probably have a new woman in your bed every night."

The tilt of his lips grew. "Sometimes two."

She sucked in a gasp. Why she had even said such a thing, she did not know, but she could not have him focusing on her vulnerability at present. It was far easier to deflect the attention back to him.

"W-will you just turn your back while I dress?"

He stared at her for too long. It made her skin itch as his gaze ran over her from head to toe. Finally, he nodded. He moved into the corner of the room and turned to face the wall. "Tell me when you're done."

Hannah hastily tugged open her travelling bag and pulled out a dry dress and shift. She eyed the door to goodness knows where and knew she had little choice. There was no chance she would go into one of the other rooms alone. The mere thought made her shudder.

She stripped quickly, pausing to glance at Red's back. He remained facing the wall, his arms folded across his chest, an image of pure masculine power—strong in stance, with his wide shoulders silhouetted by the damp linen of his shirt.

She snorted to herself. Masculine power? What nonsense. She pulled the shift over her head. Her stays were damp too, but there was little that could be done about that. Hopefully she would warm with a dry shift and dress on.

Hannah tugged her dress on and gave a wriggle. The fabric remained bunched around her head. She cursed. She forgot it had extra buttons on the back in her haste. She should have undone them first. Practically blinded by the bunched dress, she gave another wriggle and tried to drag her arms free.

Blast.

"Um..." She pulled her arm from the sleeve, but it caught at her elbow and pinched into her skin. "Um...Red?"

"Yes?"

She couldn't see if he had turned to look at her muddle yet. She had to assume he had not or else he would surely fall into a laughing fit. Oh what a mess she had to look. Soaked, half-naked, and trapped by her own gown.

"C-could you help me?"

His spluttered laugh told her he'd finally turned. She waited, her head still covered by the dress, her arms at an awkward angle above head.

"Well?" she demanded, aware of heat in her cheeks and likely the rest of her. At least she did not have to worry about catching a chill anymore.

"How did this happen?"

"There are several buttons on the back. I forgot to undo them and now...well, now I am stuck," she explained, her voice muffled.

His fingers on her back made her jump. "Stand still," he ordered.

She tried but was far too aware of this touch. No one but maids had ever helped her dress. Most days she did it herself, as she and her father never took servants with them on their travels. Honestly, why she was utterly unable to dress herself today of all days, she did not know.

"Hannah," he scolded when she twitched at the feel of his fingers near her spine.

A few more torturous moments later and he had the dress pulled over her head and down. She lowered her arms and found herself staring into his eyes that were made all the more intense by the low shadows. Her heart gave an erratic beat. Then another. Then she was sure it stopped.

She continued to stare—as did he. It was the oddest moment, for although she was no longer bound in her dress, she could hardly move, hardly breathe. All from looking into his eyes. Perhaps it was the way his gaze kept dropping briefly to her lips, or maybe it was because she had never seen a man so handsome.

He stepped closer and the desire to shrink back and escape the intensity of his presence screamed through her, but her legs hadn't figured out how to work. She shivered.

"Turn around." His voice was a harsh whisper. "I'll do your buttons."

Meekly, she did as she was told. Red brushed aside some damp hair and another shiver wracked her at the feel of his fingers upon the nape of her neck.

"Are you still cold?"

She nodded, though in truth, she could hardly tell. Her skin was ice-like that much she knew, yet her body felt aflame and far too aware of him so close to her. She could lean back, and they would be touching, body to body. Now why was that so tempting? She had never been aware of a man physically before. Ever. Why now? Why with Red?

He finished the buttons and put his hands to her shoulders to turn her around. "Do you have a dry pelisse? Or a spencer? I'll start a fire, but this place won't stay that warm, not with the broken windows. I have my doubts there is anything else in here that will keep us warm." He jerked his head upward. "There was a hole in the roof. Any beds will be ruined, but I'll check shortly."

She nodded, legs still frozen. When he moved away, it was a miracle she did not puddle on the floor as though the ice in her had thawed and left her as nothing but liquid.

"Well?" he prompted when she had not moved.

"Yes, of course." She jumped into motion, riffling through her bag until she came up with a spencer. She pulled it on and did up the buttons. While she was there, she also tugged out some gloves and added them to her outfit. They did not match but at least her numb fingers might warm quicker. She eyed Red's white shirt, still stuck to his back and revealing far too much as he set about sorting out the tinder. "Will you not change?"

He shrugged. "I'll dry soon enough."

Hannah frowned. "You will get sick."

"I never get sick."

"Nonsense, everyone gets sick."

He glanced at her long enough to grin. "Not me."

Red stood and picked up one of the abandoned chairs. He threw it to the floor and the furniture made a cracking sound. Then he kicked it several times. Wood splintered and the old chair broke apart.

She blinked at this show of strength but refused to let herself be anyway intrigued by it. After all, if she tried hard enough, she could certainly break a chair. There was nothing at all exciting about such a display. Nothing at all.

"Nothing at all."

"Pardon?"

She smiled hastily. "Nothing."

At a loss as for what to do, Hannah drew up her shoulders and forced herself to properly confront their lodgings for the night. She still would not venture any farther into the building, but she should at least acquaint herself with their surroundings.

She twisted to eye the bar, its long length so barren. Once upon a time, men would have come here after a long journey and sit at it until their bodies were warm and relaxed with alcohol. More tables and chairs would have occupied the space and it would have smelled of cigarette smoke and warm pies. Now it was nothing more than a shell—a ghostly, dark, damp shell.

She turned her attention back to Red. Perhaps acquainting herself with the room was not the best idea. The only non-spooky thing in the room was the smuggler. What a pickle she was in when he was the most constant thing in her world.

In her perusal, she did spot another tiny stump of a candle and an old lamp. She lit the stump from the lone candle and drew up the wick of the lamp. She gave it a little shake and was pleased to hear there was a little liquid left in it. After a few tries, she got it lit and placed it in one of the darkened corners. The cozy light took away some of the spookiness at least.

Once Red had managed to get the fire going, the idea of spending the night in the abandoned inn was a little less daunting. It crackled invitingly, and he urged her to come close, drawing over a chair and motioning for her to sit in it.

"I shall explore—see if I can find anything that will make our stay more comfortable. You remain here."

Hannah nodded. Silently she cursed herself. She was meant to be the one in charge here. Instead she had spent the entire evening nodding like a puppet.

Logically, there was no reason to be scared by an old building except perhaps the stability of the structure, but buildings like this were built to last. It had likely been on this spot for several hundred years and would remain so for another hundred. There was nothing of which to be scared.

But when Red left her, her breathing grew shallow. She focused on the dancing flames of the fire, forcing herself not to look deep into every shadow or listen to the howling wind. She gripped the arms of the chair tight and cautioned herself to breathe.

Deep breaths. *One, two, three.* She froze. What was that? A crack. Followed by a thud. Had something terrible happened to Red? What if he had fallen through the ceiling? Or a beam had come down upon him? She jolted upright, knocking over her chair. She tugged open the door he had gone out of and barreled into the darkness.

CHAPTER NINE

Red had hardly been prepared for the woman flying at him anymore than he'd expected to do battle with a sizeable rat. The bloody thing had taken quite the exception to Red invading his lodgings and had run at him with such force, he'd been forced to jump aside and nearly fallen through a hole in the floor.

He grabbed Miss St. John and held her back from him.

"Are you well?" she asked, her breaths rapid.

He nodded. As well as he could be anyway. She could have little idea the sight of her nipples pressing against the cotton of her shift was now burned into his brain. Or that the generous swells of her breasts and hips had been singed on the inside of his eyelids. This now meant, unfortunately, that he was seeing Miss St. John in an entirely different light.

Well, perhaps he had been mildly aware of her attractiveness, and he had certainly found himself a little too fascinated by the annoying bluestocking. But she had not aroused him until now.

She stared up at him. There was enough light seeping through from the broken windows above and the hole in the roof for him to see her features clearly enough. Her eyes glinted and her lips pursed. Her rapid breathing drew his attention inevitably down to her chest.

"I thought..." She sucked in a breath, forcing her breasts to rise against her gown.

He groaned inwardly.

"I thought you were hurt."

He shook his head again.

"That crash..."

He shook his head once more. Miss St. John finally fell silent. Perhaps the weight of his attraction to her had finally fallen upon her and shut her up. He could not decide whether to be grateful or not. At least when she was talking incessantly, he was less likely to think of kissing her. Or was he? A kiss would silence her to be certain.

She swayed into him a little. Whatever the heck this was, she was struggling too. He was not unaware women found him handsome, though his wealth would have made him attractive no matter how much he looked like the rear end of a farm animal. However, he could hardly have expected a woman like Miss St. John to be attracted to him. Hell, the woman thoroughly disapproved of him, and he had little inclination to change that.

But those lips that were usually pressed into a firm line were slightly parted and far too full. Far too tempting.

Damn and blast, this was not what he had intended at all.

"Red?"

The word tripped over his spine, jumping over each notch and making him shudder. Never had his nickname sounded so sensual.

"Hannah."

For God's sakes, why did he say that?

He closed the gap, drawing her close to his damp chest. And why the hell did he do that? There would be no benefit to kissing this uptight woman. The sooner he had her off his hands, the better. If he kissed her, she might expect more from him. Heck, she was likely so inexperienced, she'd expect a marriage proposal or something awful like that.

Spreading his palms over her back, he relished the feel of her body against his. She stared up at him as though entranced. The groans he'd been keeping in escaped. The rise and fall of her breasts against him sent his mind hazy.

He leaned in, felt her breaths against his lips.

Miss St. John screamed. She tore from him and barreled into the other room. When he finally gathered his senses and slowed his racing heart, he followed her in to find her curled up on the chair near the fire, her legs hugged tightly to her.

"Well, I know I should not have done that, but there was no need to scream."

"It was not...it was no that. Something...something ran across my foot."

Red pinched his brow. That blasted rat. Though he supposed he ought to be grateful to it from saving him from making a big mistake.

"There's nothing in here. You can put your feet down."

She twisted in the chair and carefully inspected every corner. Lowering her feet, she narrowed her eyes at him. "If anything touches me again, I am sleeping outside."

"And here I thought you were a practical woman."

"I am. Being...wary of unknown creatures is extremely practical. One does not know what they might do to one."

"It was just a rodent."

"A disease carrying rodent! I would rather freeze to death than catch a disease from a rat."

He heaved a sigh and dragged over another chair. Hopefully it had enough strength in it to hold him up.

They watched the flames in silence for some time. Red stood to give the fire a poke with the wooden leg he'd kept as a poker. He glanced at Miss St. John and a smile tugged from him. Mouth open, she was still bundled up, safe from rats, but fast asleep.

He eyed the thin muslin of her gown and noted the tremor gently rumbling through her body. Her hair had dried, leaving it in wild, bouncy curls around her face. The temptation to pull one and wrap it around his finger was strong—too strong. Why should he care what her hair felt like? He already knew what her body felt like, after all—soft, warm, supple. Mere hair should not interest him.

He rose and snatched up his greatcoat. It had dried well and the wool was thick enough to keep out most of the rain. With careful steps, he edged over to the sleeping woman and laid the garment over her, tucking it up around her chin. She made a sleepy sound but did not open her eyes. He tilted his head to eye the innocent vision she made.

Innocent. Wholly and utterly innocent. And a royal pain in the arse. Nothing appealing here at all and yet...and yet he could not help admire the relaxed shape of her lips or the way her dark lashes skimmed her cheeks. Those little freckles too—they were interesting. He wanted to sweep his finger over her nose and trace them then perhaps see if she had more on her body.

Fool.

He would not be seeing any freckles or any more of Miss St. John's body. He would find them transport at the next town and be on their way, and he would not touch her again nor would he think of anything other than getting rid of that blasted stone and returning home to continue the smuggling operation. There was much to be done, and he didn't much like being left out of the excitement.

Just before he backed off, a tingle started in his nose. He tried to catch it but too late. A sneeze wracked him, and Miss St. John startled away, bolting up from the chair and bringing her forehead into direct contact with his chin. His teeth rattled in his jaw, and a bolt of pain seared through him. She cried out and slumped back into the chair.

Red staggered back a few steps, clutching his jaw. "God, you have a hard head," he muttered.

The tang of blood told him he'd suffered some damage. He prodded his mouth with a finger and discovered he's managed to cut his bottom lip on his teeth. He grimaced as he withdrew the bloodied finger.

"You're hurt?" she declared, rising.

He held up a hand. "Don't bloody move." He was not quite sure he trusted her to be near him. "Are you harmed?"

She shook her head. "I do have a hard head," she admitted.

A reluctant smile escaped him.

"What were you doing?"

He rescued his coat from the floor. "Attempting to keep you warm." He offered it to her.

"Do you not need it? You sneezed."

"One sneeze. It hardly means anything."

"I pray it does not. I would not wish you blaming me for your illness." She snuggled under his coat.

"I will not get ill," he said confidently. And if he did, he would be blaming it on that blasted stone.

CHAPTER TEN

No matter how many times Hannah yawned or rubbed her eyes, she could not rid herself of the fog brought on by lack of sleep. She peered at the bright sunshine that split the clouds for a moment before vanishing again. At least the weather had dried up and the clouds were white and fluffy with little threat of rain. The white puffs cast shadows over the headland that stretched out in front of them.

She and Red had ventured out in the early hours, both unable to sleep after their adventures the previous night. He strode ahead, following the worn grooves left by the carriages that ventured along the coast. Here the cliffs didn't drop but rather rolled down a steep slope to the sea. Beneath, the waves washed over a sandy beach. A chill was still in the air, but it did not stop her wanting to slip down the hill and bury her feet in the sand and perhaps even close her eyes and sleep the day away.

However, the stone that Red carried forced away thoughts of relaxing and catching up on sleep. They had to get it to safety before anything else happened. With the luck they were having, she feared it might end up damaged or lost or something else terrible. The plan was to find transport at the next town then hopefully make enough progress to sleep in a more comfortable inn tonight.

Red strode ahead with the stone tucked under one arm. His greatcoat was slung over one shoulder, and he carried his luggage with ease. She envied the strength in those broad shoulders and arms. It frustrated her that she needed to rely on a man to help her with the stone.

Those arms...

A sigh escaped her. She scowled at herself. She had never, ever sighed over a man.

It didn't help she now understood fully the strength in those arms. Hannah's frown deepened. Did it matter if he was strong? Did it matter if it felt absurdly good to be in this arms? Why should she care about such things? It wasn't logical. She enjoyed intellect in men and manners and... well not strength and arrogance and the many other traits that made up Red.

"Miss St. John?"

She realized she had slowed her pace to almost nothing in her contemplative state. She hastened to catch up.

"Are you tired?"

Hannah shook her head and clamped her jaw shut as she fought an encroaching yawn.

"We're only about three miles from town. It should not take us long."

She heard his unspoken words—*if she kept up with him.*

"I am perfectly well, I promise. I will not hold you up."

"Never fear, Miss St. John, we shall have you in a comfortable carriage before long."

"You have me marked as a pampered woman, do you not? Surely it is you who is the pampered one, considering your position?"

"An heir to a title is never pampered, let me assure you of that. He's forced to grow up very quickly."

"So you did not live a comfortable life?"

He smirked. "Comfortable, yes. I have every benefit afforded to me by wealth and do not think I am not aware of that, Miss St. John. However, a first son is cast into the flames as soon as he's able to walk."

"You make it sound as though your childhood was hard." She eyed his profile, aware she was being thoroughly rude with her curiosity, but considering his behavior so far and the various...er...situations they had been in, she was fairly certain they were past worrying about manners.

Besides, he fascinated her. People seldom did. She was much more interested in history and the evidence of it left behind for people to discover than the fickleness of individuals. However, Red was entirely unlike anyone she had ever met.

Her father was connected with several high-ranking men of society through his studies, and it was not unusual for them to have an earl or a viscount over for dinner at their manor house. She might only be the daughter of a baron, but she had experienced plenty of time in the company of men like Red.

And yet they were so unlike him.

She wanted to study this new specimen. Understand him better.

For purely scientific purposes of course.

"My father was an excellent man. My brother and I were content and well-looked after. I merely mean to point out that it is not all a bed of roses being the heir to a title."

"If your life was so excellent, why turn to crime?"

He stilled and threw her an amused look. "And here I thought you had forgotten what I was for a moment."

"Did you wish me to?"

"Not at all," he said, his voice deadpan. "But you are terribly fond of ordering me about like a servant. I had wondered if you had forgotten my fearsome reputation."

She clutched her bag to her. "Are you trying to scare me?"

"If I was, there would be little point now. We are stuck together, Miss St. John, for better or worse, until this blasted stone is gone."

"Good. Because you don't."

He glanced at her again, amusement tugging up his lips.

Hannah almost hated that look. It was patronizing and frustrating. She was not here to amuse him nor was she here as some silly little girl who could not possibly understand his way of life. She had been in the adult world for quite some time and had experienced a lot of life through her father. Why, he had trusted her to fend for herself since she was a girl of three and ten as he travelled the world. She was not some innocent chit who knew nothing of life.

"I think I could scare you if I wished." He paused to place down the stone, readjust the wrapping, and move his bag to his other arm.

"Fear is illogical. It is based on the unknown. Humans fear change and difference, and things we do not understand. All one needs to do is take the time to study what it is one fears and inevitably the fear vanishes."

"Like rats? Have you studied rats?"

She lowered her bag and gave her arms a little stretch. "I do not have a fear of rats, but they are disease-carrying creatures. Of course I do not want one running around the same room as me. That is entirely logical."

"Logical...illogical...do you ever feel something without weighing up if it is rational of you to do so?"

"Of course. I am human, after all."

Red's gaze flickered over her face, landing briefly on her lips. Fleetingly but long enough for her to notice the action.

That same thick air had followed them over the hills. It swirled about them like a current, which was ridiculous because there should only be the fresh breeze coming from the sea, ripe with salt and seaweed. Instead, as he took one step closer, they were blanketed in a hot current. It made her skin warm and her cheeks heat, her mouth dry and her limbs heavy.

As he took another step, bringing them almost chest to chest, she lifted her gaze and felt her eyelids flutter. Her heart beat so fiercely it was like war drum. Surely the whole of Cornwall could hear it and would come running to her aid at any moment? Just exactly what was he doing?

He jerked forward suddenly, as though he was about to land his lips upon hers and a sound escaped her. What that sound was, she could hardly say. A squeak like a mouse perhaps, or even a sort of an *oh* sound. Whatever it was, it had been what he wanted.

Red took two steps back and gathered the stone. "You are scared of me."

She ran her tongue across her dry lips. "I am not." Her words were breathy.

But true. Entirely and completely true. That was not fear making her jolt or release nonsensical sounds. Terror did not make her body feel as though it had separated from her and she was no longer in control. She had seen the evidence and weighed it in her mind. She was wildly attracted to this inappropriate man.

"If you say so." He gave a knowing grin, except she was certain he had little idea what was really behind her reaction, and she had no intention of admitting to anything either.

If it served his ego to believe he intimidated her, let him believe it. All she needed from the Earl of Redmere was some strong arms and protection. Did it matter if he mistook her desire for something else?

No. And it was probably better that he did. After all, he was a smuggler, known across Cornwall for his criminal ways. Who knew what he would do if he understood she had hoped he would follow through on his threat and kiss her?

"Are you done now?" she demanded. "We have little time to waste."

He hefted up the stone and nodded. "Come then, Miss St. John. I will do your bidding once more."

"I am paying you," she reminded him. "Handsomely."

He snorted. "I could bring in more money with another shipment and in half the time."

"The money is important to you? Is your estate so very expensive to run?"

"You really are a bold woman, are you not? Did your father never teach you that such matters are not for women's ears."

"Never. He always taught me to ask questions, regardless of my sex. A quiet woman never learns anything."

"A quiet woman never gets thrown off a cliff either," he muttered.

Hannah ignored the grumbled threat. If he was only used to meek and mild ladies, it was about time he met someone who was not intimidated by him. "My father never had time for the ridiculous rules of society and neither do I."

"You mean he never took the time to teach you them."

"It is true he was an extremely busy man. If I could not accompany him, I remained at home. But I certainly do not think I missed out on anything by being encouraged to speak up and ask questions."

"Marriage," Red said.

"Pardon?"

"You will likely miss out on marriage."

Hannah laughed. "From what I can see, there is little to be

missed out on. Why would I want a man who wishes me to be silent and stupid as my husband?"

"All women want marriage, do they not? I cannot think you are that different from the rest of your sex, Miss St. John."

"Just as all earls want an heir, I suppose, and yet you do not have one."

"I haven't had the time to find a wife."

"Or the inclination."

He chuckled. "Perhaps."

"Of course, I cannot imagine many women will want to marry a smuggler, titled or not."

"You take a great deal of interest in my affairs, Hannah."

Her name on his lips sent a shiver down her spine. "As do you with mine, my lord." She emphasized the last two words, drawing them out pointedly. "But if we are to spend over a week in each other's company, I see no harm in getting to know one another."

"I think you're simply a curious chit. You cannot fool me that you genuinely want to get to know me."

"Curiosity is not a bad thing. If it were not for curiosity, you would still be living in a drafty old castle instead of a stately home with nothing but tallow candles for company."

"Curiosity is not an attractive trait in women."

She gave him a pointed look. "You sound just like an etiquette book."

"Well my governess shall be pleased. Perhaps something sank in all those years ago. However, I will concede that curiosity is not always a bad thing. Unless it is coming from a determined woman after my fortune and my title."

"Well you need not fear. I am after neither."

He stopped and glanced her over. "Excellent. Then you may ask me anything you like."

"Why smuggling? Are you truly poor? When did you

start? Does anyone else know about it? Are you not scared you will get caught?"

Red's laughter caused her to stop. "Anything else?"

"Absolutely. But that will do for now."

"I am not poor. I purchased the ship some three years ago. Once I'd gathered my crew, we began trading within a few months. Small shipments at first, but they have become larger of late. Louisa, the innkeeper, knows of our activities. There may be a few others, but they benefit well enough to keep quiet. To most people in Penshallow, I am entirely respectable. And no, I am not scared."

"Because they will never hang an earl?"

"Well, that too but there are other reasons."

"What other reasons?"

He sighed. "You know what, Miss St. John..." He held up a hand. "Hannah. I have wearied of your questions. Perhaps we can concentrate on getting to the next town, and when I am rested, I will answer some more."

Hannah scowled and opened her mouth to press further but closed it at his dark look. There was more to this smuggling than simply gaining riches, that was clear, but what was it and would he let her in on the secret? The facts about Red did not all align and more than anything, she wanted to know why.

CHAPTER ELEVEN

B y Red's calculations, they were about two miles from
town. The lazy swirls of smoke rose from the tiled
rooftops of the town nestled into the hills around the mouth
of the river. His arms had to be at least two feet longer after
carrying the blasted rock all morning so he was mightily glad
the town was in sight.

And that Hannah had quietened her questions for the
moment.

He was well aware they would start again soon. She was
simply too inquisitive for her own good. He hardly owed her
any explanations for his business dealings, but there was
something in her bright, quizzing eyes and eager tone that
made him want to tell her all. And ask all those questions in
return. How exactly did a bluestocking get tangled up in
rescuing artifacts? Did the rest of her family not mind her
unladylike behavior? Was there no one to counsel her on the
dangers of curiosity?

Not that he really thought there was anything dangerous
about a woman with a curious mind. The few intelligent
women he had met had been entirely delightful. There were

many more of them out there, no doubt, but they had been quashed by society and molded until silent. How was it Hannah had escaped unscathed and unguarded?

"Can we stop?"

He continued on. "Not far now," he announced. "I'll have you on a carriage in no time." His back gave a twinge. *And the bloody rock.*

"Red," she called from behind.

"Come now, I know you're not tired. There's no sense in resting now."

"Red," she hissed, hastening to his side. "I must stop now."

He heard the demand in the *now* and was half-expecting her to stamp her foot. He sighed, stopped, lowered the rock to the ground, and swiveled to face her. "There, we are stopped. Now what?"

She peeked over at the large boulders lining their path. Several had rolled down from the tops of the hills thousands of years ago and had remained like giant's marbles, grey and smooth against the green grass.

"I need to..." Her mouth moved but he missed the rest of the words.

"Pardon?"

"I need to..." Again, she mumbled the last words.

"For Christ's sakes, what is it, Hannah?"

"I need to relieve myself!"

"Ah. Right."

She cleared her throat and tucked her fingers into her skirts. "One of those rocks perhaps..." She pointed at the largest.

"Yes. Good idea. Right, then. I'll just..." He turned his back and waited.

There was a rustle of skirts and a few footsteps. He kicked a rock and scuffed his foot against the slowly drying mud. He narrowed his gaze into the distance as the sound of a wagon approached. It made its way at a slow pace up the rise of the hill toward him. Red took a quick look behind him to see Hannah was entirely hidden, though he imagined she had heard the wagon too and was no doubt cowering in embarrassment.

The driver rolled the wagon to a slow halt, pulling back on the reins of a rather tired-looking nag.

The driver fared no better. He removed his hat and revealed a few wisps of grey hair stubbornly clinging to his head. Pock marks littered his face and his clothing had been darned and re-darned until there was likely nothing left of the old garments.

"Going to town?" the stranger asked.

Red nodded stiffly.

"I can give you a ride."

"There's no need, thank you."

The man clambered down from the wagon and rubbed his chin, weighing Red up. It would be clear to the man that Red was no pauper, even without his fine carriage or well-bred horses. Red tightened his muscles and bunched his fists.

"Looks like you've come a way. There are no inns on this path. Let me help you. It will only cost...five shillings."

Red laughed. "I need no help and certainly not at that cost."

"That's a shame." The man moved more swiftly than Red could have expected from his angled, skinny frame, and drew a knife out from the back of his trousers. "I'd have been willing to leave it at a five shillings had you accepted my help."

Sighing, Red shook his head to himself. This was no high-wayman or career criminal but an opportunist. He'd seen Red's expensive attire and figured he could earn some money —legitimately or not. He prayed Hannah remained behind the rock and let him deal with the fool.

"I'll give you a shilling to be on your way. That's all you're getting."

"Red! He has a knife!"

Inwardly, he groaned as Hannah came bounding out from behind the rock. The man twisted to view her, knife held out. Red had not been scared for his own life, but when the man took a leap for her, his heart near broke through his ribs.

The would-be thief snatched her arm and pulled her close. Red moved swiftly, hardly aware of what he was doing. The artifact was heavy but not enough to prevent him from lifting it up high and bringing it down on the man's head. His head made a sickly hollow thudding sound and the man crumbled in an instant. Hannah stepped back, her eyes wide, and swung her gaze between Red and the man.

"Is he dead?"

He lowered the artifact to the ground and kicked aside the knife the thief had dropped. He pressed a finger to his neck and felt a faint pulse. There was a little blood matting his hair and signs of a nasty bump was already revealing itself.

"He's alive. Just. He'll awaken mightily sore. Might not even remember what happened."

"I cannot believe you did that."

Red stood and shrugged. "I only did what any man would do. I wouldn't have let him harm you."

"I meant with the artifact. I cannot believe you hit him with it." She hastened over to the stone and unwrapped it, skimming her fingers over it. "It isn't damaged, thank goodness."

Eyeing her for several moments, he shook his head. "You were very nearly damaged yourself, you bloody woman. Why did you not stay hidden?"

She peered up at him as though he had just spoken gibberish. "And let you be harmed?"

"Well—"

"Who would carry the stone for me?"

He set his jaw. "I am so glad you are concerned for my welfare," he said dryly.

A hint of a smile curved her lips as she stood after rewrapping the stone. "You were very brave. I'm glad you were not harmed."

"And you were very reckless. Next time, stay hidden."

"Do you think there will be a next time?"

"I hope not, but with our luck right now, I would not be surprised if we run into every highwayman in England before we reach London."

CHAPTER TWELVE

Red had said they could not take the thief's wagon unfortunately which meant by the time they had caught a stagecoach to St Austell, her feet and back were sore. The wagon would have only saved them some two miles, but he'd told Hannah it was likely stolen and they would not want to drive through the town with a stolen horse. Besides the horse was an old withered thing. Better to let the man awaken and travel on his way, Red had said.

Hannah folded her arms and lowered her chin. Red was giving a lot of orders. It should not bother her. After all, what else was he here for but to get her safely to London? Admittedly the journey had not been as smooth as she had hoped so far, but they were both safe, tucked into the stagecoach on their way once more and after all, she was no weak lady. She had climbed mountains with her father. A few miles on foot were nothing.

The day was wearing on so that the confines of the coach grew shadowed. She could not see the woman opposite so much as hear and smell her. Hannah had observed her well enough earlier to know that the noise came from heavy silk skirts and feathers atop her head. And the scent was symptomatic of her being too liberal with her scent—a deep, musky fragrance that she supposed was likely recommended for older ladies but was not pleasant to anyone.

In Hannah's own muddy gown with no fragrance or plumes of feathers, she hardly looked like she belonged in the stagecoach. Were it not for Red, they likely would not have let her board. Somehow the man looked every bit the gentleman, in spite of their adventures.

The other gentleman travelling with them—the woman's husband, she assumed—dressed as well as Red, albeit in a slightly neater fashion. Their three children had started the journey rambunctious, throwing themselves about the seats until they were too tired to do anything other than slump onto their parents' laps.

She glanced at Red's profile, his expression uninterested and vague. He showed no signs of tiredness outwardly, but she suspected by the occasional movement in his body, he was feeling as stiff and as sore as she.

The occupants of the carriage exhaled a combined sigh of relief as they drew into the town, and the stagecoach came to a stop outside the coaching inn. The link-boys dashed out, holding out their lit torches and allowing them all to exit the coach easily in the darkening evening. Next came a bustle of movement as a maid clambered down from on top of the coach and the driver and footman began unloading the luggage. Hannah had insisted the stone remain with them so they only had to collect their meagre bags before finding themselves a room.

Having only existed on a light meal at the last town, her stomach grumbled at the scent of cooked food as they entered the inn. She ducked under one very low beam and glanced back to see Red do the same, although he had to force himself much lower.

"Let us find a room, then we shall eat."

She nodded, happy with the plan and too weary to comment. Red arranged for a room, declaring them to be brother and sister before requesting a private dining room. She did find herself the subject of a quick glance over which was quickly distilled by Red handing over a sizeable sum of money for their best service. The innkeeper tucked it quickly away into his stained apron and handed over a key. He leaned in.

"We've got a washer woman who can have that dress cleaned," he hissed. "She's as good as any you'll find in town."

Red nodded and thanked the man. Hannah's cheeks flamed. She must look worse than she thought. Her mortification lasted even as Red unlocked the door to a modest-sized room with two beds that were neatly made with blankets and surprisingly fluffy pillows. Two windows looked over the courtyard. She looked out and saw the men stowing away the stagecoach and unhitching the horses for the night. She rather envied them already being tucked away in a stable and brushed down. Goodness knows, her hair likely needed a good brush, and she certainly desired a quick wash,

Red arranged their bags and lit the candles upon the fireplace before propping the stone up against one wall. The low eaves of the roof forced him to duck throughout most of this. "I'll get a maid to light the fire once we eat. It is a cold night." He motioned up and down her. "Do you wish to change?"

"That is very diplomatic of you."

"It is?"

"Well, it's a polite way of saying I am an utter mess and in need of clean clothes."

"You are in need of clean clothes." He ran his gaze over her. "But you are not an utter mess."

She puffed a breath over her face in an attempt to dispel the heat in her cheeks that had not left since the innkeeper had commented on her appearance. The hint of a smile on Red's generous mouth made her insides buckle. Gone was any hunger, replaced with the oddest warm, bubbling sensation.

She turned away before he could see her embarrassment. "If you give me a moment, I shall wash and join you downstairs."

He nodded and stepped out wordlessly. She hastened over to the wash bowl resting on a washstand lined with blue and white tiles and poured out some water. Resisting the urge to dunk her head into it, she splashed some of the cool water over her face and chest and drew in a long breath. She peeked into the mirror above and grimaced. Considering the candle-light was flattering, she looked terrible. What she would look like in full daylight, she did not want to consider.

Hannah took the time to wash her body and change into her last clean gown. The one from the previous night was crinkled and stained from the rain and mud. She hoped this washer woman was as good as the innkeeper had implied.

Slinging the garment over a chair, she moved more quickly as her stomach began to rumble again. That was better. At least she understood what a rumble meant. Far better than that oddly warm sensation in her stomach. She might find Red attractive. Handsome even. She might like the idea of kissing him. However, she did not like her body reacting in ways that she could not control. It was entirely without reason that the disagreeable man should make her stomach do such things.

At least when she joined him in the private dining room, she felt a little more in control with her hair neatened and a clean gown on.

Well, she did for a moment. One brief, lovely moment.

That was, until he smiled at her. Until his gaze ran from her slippers to her carefully pinned up hair. Until his eyes softened.

Then the warm sensation was back with vengeance. It no longer lingered in her stomach but flowed through her, making her feel as though she had just drunk a large quantity of wine. Her limbs were soft and no longer part of her. How she covered the distance between the door and the table, she did not know. When she dropped into the chair, she felt as though she weighed more than a stallion.

"I have ordered food. I hope you don't mind."

Her stomach growled, and she put a hand over it, as though that might stop it.

He chuckled. "I guess you do not."

She smiled away her embarrassment. "It has been a long day."

"And we have not eaten much," he finished. "I am glad to be out of that coach." He smothered a yawn. "If I ever have children, remind me not to travel anywhere with them. Ever."

"It cannot be much fun for them, but they were exhausting."

"Likely because they're not used to their parents disciplining them."

"No, neither of them seemed to have any say over them. They are likely always with a governess and a nanny."

"I had both, but I certainly knew to listen to my father."

Hannah tilted her head to better view the softness that lingered on his face as he spoke of his father. It was one of the few times his lips were not quirked in arrogance or disdainful amusement. "He must have been a good father."

"The best. He was not one to relinquish his duties to others. He took a daily interest in my brother and me."

"I had both a nanny and a governess, but I will confess I did not find much use for a governess. When I was twelve, my fifth governess declared me unteachable and left."

"Unteachable?"

"I corrected her one time too many." Hannah chuckled as she recalled the woman's face dropping in horror as once more, an admittedly pretentious twelve-year-old proved her wrong. She could not deny she still had her moments when she could not help but speak up and correct people, but she was much better at doing it without causing offence these days.

"So you were too clever for them," he commented. "Your father travelled a lot, you said. How did you occupy yourself when he was away?"

"I learned to run the house and of course studied when I could. Father would bring home new books and artifacts all the time. I'm sure I learned more in those years than all the years previous. Sometimes I would be allowed to go with him but usually only to Scotland or Wales."

The warmer memories faded somewhat as she recalled begging her father not to go. She understood his need to find out more, she really did. She could hardly claim to be any less hungry for knowledge, but at the same time, she had so longed for more time with her father. There had to be a better way of balancing it, surely?

The bang of a door jolted her from such thoughts, and she focused on the servant as she brought in two bowls of stew with a great, big wedge of bread on the side. Any thoughts of her father or angry governesses fled as she dipped her spoon into the steaming bowl and brought juicy chunks of beef and carrots to her mouth. Hannah took a delicate sip, only to see Red watching her with mild amusement.

"What is it?"

"There is no need for manners. We are both ravenous, and I can assure you, I intend to eat like a beast." He tore a chunk of bread off, dunked it in the stew and shoved it into his mouth, grinning around the piece as he chewed.

Hannah tentatively tore off a piece of bread too, her stomach giving a squeeze at the feel of soft bread and crumbling crust. She dipped it into the stew and took a bite. When Red's face did not turn into a mask of disgust, she became bolder and took a bigger bite. A groan escaped her.

The way Red's eyes flared startled her. She could not be sure why it happened but his expression turned into something other than amusement, though who knew what it was. Sometimes she wished she had spent less time studying history and more time studying human emotions. At least she would understand people better.

Casting her gaze down, she concentrated on the food until she could be sure his face had turned back to normal. When she looked up again, he was tucking into the bread and stew as though it might vanish it at any moment.

She giggled.

"What is it?"

"If anyone had told me a few weeks ago that I would be eating with an earl—a smuggling earl, no less—and that he was going to be eating like an utter beast, I would have called them a liar."

"Well if anyone had told me I would be trekking across the country carrying a stone with an attractive bluestocking, I would have also called them a liar."

Hannah opened her mouth but whether to protest the bluestocking or attractive part she did not know. She was hardly a ravishing beauty nor was she a beast, and she conceded she was entirely bluestocking material. If that put her in leagues with informed, intelligent women, she could not complain.

When she glanced in his eyes and saw the half-smile on his lips, she knew it had all been intended as a compliment.

How odd.

CHAPTER THIRTEEN

Although the meal helped a great deal, Red could not claim to feel revived. Not when his head kept pounding and his skin fluctuated between flaming hot and ice cold. His biggest desire at present was to curl up in the rather comfortable-looking bed upstairs. Unfortunately, he had to keep the presence up for Hannah. He could hardly let her know he was not feeling at all well after declaring he never sickened. Besides, all he needed was a good night's sleep and all would be well.

Of course, his second biggest desire was Hannah at present. Why the eventful day of feral children and a near theft had made him feel any more desirous toward her, he could not say. After the scolding she gave him about using the stone as a weapon, he should be thoroughly ticked off with her.

But the meal had been pleasant, in spite of the ache in his skull, and he could not help feel he understood her that little bit better. Hannah was too smart really. No one could fully grasp her and her father, while seeming to encourage her pursuit of knowledge, had also confined her to the role of a woman too much—leaving her at home to tend to the house-keeping and the like. She needed more stimulation.

He grimaced to himself as he thanked the maid and forced his mind onto very dull things indeed.

Stimulation. He should not use that word and think of Hannah in the same moment. It summoned up ideas of how he might stimulate her. And he certainly was not thinking of her mind. Hell, the image of her nipples prodding against her chemise was still implanted into his brain. That memory and looking at her in the candlelight, her curls not quite perfect and her lips all pursed as she studied the room had him on edge and far too likely to let his mind wander into places it should not go.

Dull things. Dull things. Dull things.

Chess. Doing the accounts. Reading Plato.

Hannah's nipples.

"Shall we?" He stood abruptly and instantly regretted it. His head swam.

She scowled at him. "Is all well?"

He eased back her chair and helped her stand. "Of course."

"It's just you...swayed."

"I certainly did not."

"You did."

He drew in a breath through his nostrils. "I did not. Now let us retreat for the night. We have a long day ahead. I'll see that your dress is cleaned for the morning."

She gave him another quizzical look. "He did sway," he heard her mutter to herself.

She made no more comment on his stance or his supposed swaying as they readied for bed. He preferred sleeping naked, but for her sake, he remained in his shirt. He turned his back while she stripped down to her chemise and dove under the covers. Red knew she dove as he caught a glimpse of a blur of white flying across the room in the window reflection and the bed gave a great creak and a heavy thud.

"Oh no."

He turned. The thud had been the bed collapsing. Now in two pieces, the mattress was entirely sagged in the middle with Hannah sat atop it. She looked up at him like a child hoping not to get into trouble with its parent. He shook his head to himself.

"It must have been a weak bed," she declared.

That, and she had been so keen to hide herself from him. Not that he could blame her. Of their two nights they had been together, fifty percent of them had been him trying to kiss her. Hannah was no fool. She knew well what he intended.

He would have to up his record and not turn it into one hundred percent attempted kisses.

"I had better see if there is another room, though the innkeeper said another coach had come in. I doubt there are any more doubles, and I do not much like the thought of putting you in a room on your own."

"No, it is fine. I shall just drag this mattress onto the floor..." She clambered up and began trying to heft it over.

Red strode over and urged her aside so he could move the mattress away from the wreckage of the bed. "You sleep in that bed. I'll sleep here."

"Oh, you do not need to..."

His head pounded urgently. "Hannah, do not argue with me."

She clamped her mouth shut and with much, much more caution, climbed into the bed intended for him. He would sleep on a rock for all he cared, his body was so tired, but he could not have her sleeping on the floor, mattress or not.

He waited until she settled then blew out the candles. The

maid had set up a fire that glowed brightly enough to enable him to find his way back to the mattress. It also meant he could view Hannah all tucked up far too easily.

It was a good job he was so exhausted really. She made a very tempting proposition. Odd really, because there was little that could be thought of as sensual or sexual about a woman in a long chemise, curled up on her side, the blankets tucked up under her chin.

And yet...

He released what had to be his hundredth frustrated sigh of the evening.

Yet there was something about her.

She watched him climb onto the mattress. His cock stirred so he quickly tucked the blanket around himself and silently had a word with his manhood. Never had he had such a problem with control and especially not over bundles of bluestocking women.

He closed his eyes and focused on the blackness behind them. Even though he was fairly certain he had never been as tired as this before in his entire life, the urge to flick open his eyelids and watch her sleep was fierce. Which was ridiculous. What sort of an idiot watched women sleep? What on earth would Hannah think if she awoke to find him staring at her?

The thought of terrifying the woman who had done nothing more than look far too attractive in her matronly chemise forced him to keep his eyes shut. He felt every lump of the floor through the too-thin mattress and heard the pop and snap of the fire along with the bluster of wind occasionally breezing through a gap in the window. He cracked open an eye and peered around at the interior, lit by the orange glow of the fire. He looked everywhere but Hannah.

Her soft breaths rattled his brain. They were slow and relaxed. She had to be asleep. Each delicate puff of air found its way directly into his brain, tangling around his thoughts and most likely turning him into a madman. He could resist no longer. He twisted his head.

A smile split his lips. Her mouth was ajar, one hand tucked under her head. Her cheek was all squished as it rested on the hand. A few wisps of hair had come loose from her braid and followed the line of her jaw. It was an entirely adorable picture.

Christ, he didn't think he'd ever used the word adorable in his life, and here he using it to refer to a woman he was becoming increasingly lecherous toward. It was that blasted stone, it had to be.

He wasn't one to believe in luck. He had always made his own. But bad luck...perhaps that existed. It would explain everything that had happened so far, from the storm to the broken bed, and perhaps was even responsible for trying to send him mad over a woman who could not be more wrong for him and was certainly not the type of lady one took to bed on a whim.

Red squeezed his eyes closed and drew his attention back to the darkness behind his lids. He took deep breaths and focused on the sound of them, counting them. *One, two, three*...Hannah's nipples...*four, five, six*...pouty lips...*seven, eight*...what would she look like naked?

He tossed to the other side and gave himself up to the thoughts. His mind was clearly not going to settle until he had fully imagined every inch of her. Perhaps it would be better to get it out of the way. Once he had done that, he would stop wondering. He closed his eyes and pictured her to his heart's content.

"Red."

He groaned at the soft sound of his name on her lips. Christ, how he wanted to hear that over and over.

"Say it again," he murmured.

"Red." It was more urgent this time.

"Again."

"Red, wake up!"

He jerked his eyes open to find Hannah next to him, all buttoned up and not naked and willing next to him as he'd been dreaming. Apparently all he had needed to fall asleep was to think of Hannah naked. He hoped it was not a permanent thing.

"Red, you are burning up."

Her palm was on his forehead. He took a full moment to analyze the state of his body and realized she was correct. Every part of him was clammy with sweat. He pushed back the blanket.

"You're sick," she declared.

"No. I never get sick."

That was when he noticed how scratchy his voice was. His throat was not exactly feeling great either. The ache that had lingered in his head had spread to his ears and throat, leaving him feeling gritty and as though his head had been filled full of sand.

"You are." She stood and he heard her pour out some water. When the wet washcloth struck his head, he cursed aloud. "Stay still. You need to cool down."

When he gave into her attentions, it was not so bad. Her soft voice was somewhat soothing and the way she touched his face made the aches ease.

"Get into my bed. You cannot sleep here."

He shook his head.

"Don't be stubborn. I need you in good health."

"Oh yes, would not want your stone-carrier to get sick. Might as well be a damned donkey," he murmured as she urged him to sit.

Hannah gave him a look. "I would not wish illness on you, even if you had decided not to help, but I will certainly not let you sicken further while in my care."

He gave into her persistent tugs and made his way to the bed. The mattress pressed against bed ropes and cradled his body much better than the one on the floor. He sighed, long and loud.

She stood over him and wrung her hands together. "I should get you some tea."

"No, just sleep. I'll have tea in the morning." He wasn't sure he could get up the energy to sit up for a hot drink. His lids were weighted with stones heavier than the damned artifact. "I'm hot," he complained.

Hannah laid the cloth over his forehead again then dabbed it against the visible skin at the opening of his shirt. He could not help regret he was too ill to enjoy it.

"How did you know?" he asked.

"Know what?"

"I was sick."

"You were muttering my name and tossing and turning." He saw her grin through his half-closed lids. "I knew you had to be sick to be saying my name."

She went to dampen the cloth and laid the frigid coldness over his head again. "I have put out the fire as best as I can and the window is open."

"You'll be cold."

"No, I'll be fine."

He knew she was lying, trying to be brave. It was something he had seen her do the previous evening, and he wondered how often she had played the courageous woman before, particularly in the face of a father who, by all accounts, left her alone since she was a young girl. He grasped her wrist when she moved away.

"Sleep here."

"I will stay by your side."

"No, I mean..." A cough bubbled up from nowhere, and he spent several minutes trying to clear his throat. "Sleep in this bed. With me. You'll stay warm and I...I would like you by my side."

It was not a lie, though it was not something he really wanted to confess to, but if it appeased her enough to get her to stay warm in his bed, he would say it.

Hannah slid onto the mattress next to him, her body rigid. Had he been in better health, other parts of him would be rigid too. She softened slowly. Her hand came to his forehead and then swept down his face. She soothed him with a gentle touch until he could feel the heaviness pulling him under. Red almost did not want to succumb. Part of him wanted to remain awake the entire night to enjoy her tender attentions.

CHAPTER FOURTEEN

Hannah's arm was useless. Utterly useless. No matter how she tried, it would not work. She pulled and lifted, but it refused to do anything. How was she meant to carry the stone now? How was she meant to look after Red? She rolled and a grunting sound issued from somewhere. Peeling open her eyes, she waited for the sleepy haze to clear before focusing her attention on her arm. No wonder she had been dreaming such odd things. Red's head rested on her arm.

She blinked again in lieu of rubbing her eyes. Her lips curved. There was something ridiculously vulnerable about him when he slept. He was almost buried against her, tucked into the crook of her arm. His dark lashes fanned across his cheeks, and the creases around his eyes were relaxed. His hair was a wild tangle of chestnut.

In spite of his relaxed state, it was clear he was still sick. Sweat clung to his skin, making it sheen, and his hair was damp too. She pressed tentative fingers to his forehead. Still hot, but his breathing was steady and not rasping. Hopefully the cold had not gone down to his chest.

She attempted to wriggle her hand free again. He grunted and rolled onto his back. Hannah yanked her hand free and tried to avert her gaze from what this new position had revealed.

It was no good. She glanced down his body. His shirt gaped, revealing more of his chest. A faint dusting of dark hair spanned it. The tiny whorls were mesmerizing.

Would they be soft to touch? She would have thought they would be coarse but they looked soft. Before she could give into the desire to touch his chest, she shifted her attention down. That was almost certainly a mistake.

His legs were uncovered, his shirt hardly covering him. Strong, thick thighs, also covered in a similar amount of hair took up the majority of the bed. His legs were so different to her own that the contrast between them shocked her. It was not that she unfamiliar with a man's body or even unaware they could be so strong and hairy and...and...well, she wanted to say beautiful, but she had never really considered the male body to be beautiful before. But she had never seen one so close or so...naked.

She forced herself up before she did anymore studying. They would not be travelling anywhere today with Red sick so she would have to nurse him back to health. Hopefully they would only be delayed by a day or so.

Hannah completed her ablutions with haste, aware Red could awake at any moment, and put on yesterday's dress. She swiped a brush through her tangled hair and braided then pinned it up. The unsettled night and the awareness of Red next to her had left her body stiff and aching. She grimaced and rubbed the knot in her back. Some of the guests would be leaving today so she would see if they could get a new room with a bed each.

Of course, he might ask her to share his bed again. Some soft, squishy part of her had been flattered and entirely unable to deny him, not while he was sick. It was strange to see this strong man vulnerable. Part of her liked it.

She glanced over him to find him watching her.

"Have you been awake long?"

He shook his head. "I woke as you were doing your hair." His voice was hoarse and sleep-filled. "You're very good at it."

She lifted her brows. "You're a hair expert?"

"You're quick."

She shrugged. "My father never kept a lady's maid. I mostly did it myself. It's more practical to be able to it by oneself anyway." She came to his bedside and touched his forehead, even though she already knew he was hot and clammy. But she liked touching him. "How do you feel?"

"Like I've been run over by a carriage."

"You do not look well. I was about to request some food be brought up. You could do with something hot and some tea or coffee."

"I can come down." He pushed himself up with a groan, but Hannah put a hand to his chest and urged him down. Had he been in better health, she knew he would not have let her, but he sagged back down.

"Damn head," he muttered. "I never get sick."

"Well, you are sick now, and if you want to get better quickly, you had better listen to me."

His lips tilted. "I have to be a good patient, is that it?"

"Yes."

"What makes you think I will not be?"

"Because I know you already, Red. You are as stubborn as they come."

"Takes one to know one."

She smiled. "Perhaps. Now lie still and do not get up until I've returned."

"Can I at least take a piss?"

Hannah narrowed her gaze at him. If he thought his

coarse language would shock her, he was severely wrong. "You may," she said primly before breezing out of the room.

She arranged for them to move rooms after lunch as well as booking another night.

"He's not contagious, is he?" the Innkeeper asked.

She shook her head. "Merely a cold. We should only need an extra night."

The man swiped his grubby hands across his apron. "If you're after transport, there won't be another mail coach until Thursday."

Two days away. "I had feared that. Perhaps we will find room on another stage. Thought I am not sure if R—my brother will be better by then anyway."

"It's all this rain. Makes people sick."

"It's silly men who refuse to tend to themselves," she muttered. "Can we have some food brought up? Porridge and some soup if you have some? And some coffee and tea?"

The innkeeper didn't appear phased by her demands, likely because they had already been generous with their tips and he would have no concern over them settling their bill. She handed over a shilling to smooth things along and collected her cleaned and pressed gown before heading back to their room.

Red must have relieved himself and sprawled back on the bed because she found him snoring, his arms spread above his head and his legs wide apart. She shifted the blanket just enough to conceal the dark shadows between his thighs that were only just covered by his shirt. It was not that she could see anything but she did not want the temptation to peek.

What a terrible person she was.

Hannah contented herself with peeling open the covering on the stone and drawing out her notepad. She began copying what she could, though there was so much text it would take some time.

Red's snores rattled through the room. At least he was resting and she was doing something useful. Once the stone was in the hands of those at the British Museum, it would be hidden away and studied by experts until it was—hopefully—deciphered. If they could understand this stone and its translations, they could unlock the key to hieroglyphs. But it did mean she might never see it again, and she would not mind her chance to study it.

A knock on the door forced her up from her position on the floor and stopped Red's snores. He muttered and tossed onto his side. Hannah rolled her eyes at the sight of too much thigh. The man was determined to reveal himself entirely to her, she was sure of it. She shifted the blanket again and opened the door to take the tray of food from the serving maid.

At the thud of the door shutting, Red awoke fully. He peered at her through half-lidded eyes. "Food?"

She nodded. "Food. You no doubt need some." Lifting a palm, she motioned for him to stay. "Tea or coffee? And there's soup and porridge as well as some bread."

"Coffee, I think."

"You should have tea. You could do with some more sleep, but it will soothe your throat."

A lone brow rose. "Tea it is then, I suppose."

"What food would you like?"

"Some bread will do for now."

She shook her head. "Eat the soup while it's hot. You can dunk some bread in. I think you should try the porridge too if you can. You need sustenance."

He eyed her. "Fine. Soup it is."

Pouring a dash of milk into the cup, she lifted the lid of the teapot to check it had brewed and added it to the cup. "Sugar?"

"No."

"You ought to. It will give you energy."

"I don't like sweet tea."

"It's not about what you like." She added a spoonful of sugar. "It is about getting you healthy." Hannah brought over the cup and ignored his stubborn scowl. Her father was the same when he was sick. Men wanted to be looked after but at the same time did not want to be told what to do. Well Red could not have it both ways.

"Drink that and then you can have the soup."

"Of course, milady, anything you say, milady."

She frowned at his mocking tone. "This is for your own good."

"I'm a grown man, Hannah, I can make my own decisions." He wrinkled his nose, and Hannah snatched the cup from him just before he sneezed and nearly spilled it everywhere.

"You are a grown, sick man. Let someone else make the decisions for a change." She handed back the cup and pulled out a handkerchief so he could blow his nose.

"I'm not sure I trust you to make my decisions. You would choose a damn stone over a man anytime."

"What makes you think I need to make such a choice?"

"I am willing to bet you have chosen studies over a man many times."

She shook her head. "I have chosen not to entertain men who do not interest me, for certain, but that does not mean I have chosen one over the other. If a man cannot interest me enough to draw me away from my studies, he must not be worth it."

He smirked. "You have many of these types of suitors I suppose."

"Hardly. I am too busy, and as you so pointed out, I am cast as a bluestocking. We do not tend to fight off men on a daily basis."

"I am sure your father entertains some interesting men."

She lifted a shoulder. "None were that interesting to me. Or they were extremely old."

"So you have fended off some suitors?" He took a long gulp of tea and handed it back to her.

Hannah retrieved the soup and waited for him to sit up. She passed him the bowl and added a chunk of bread to it. "There were one or two men who thought I would make an excellent wife, perhaps because of what I do for my father."

"Ah. To an intellectual, you are probably the perfect wifely material."

She tried not to be offended at the indication that he did not think her perfect wifely material for anyone else, but why should she care? She had no intention of marrying and leaving her father.

"I have little idea of their motivations to pursue me. Nevertheless, I would not marry so easily. I think I would rather not marry at all."

"They want a pretty little thing to nod and agree with their theories and be willing to follow them about as they dig for stones or whatever it is these men do."

He was not wrong. Her intellect and interest in the past had appealed to a couple of her father's friends. It was not that she did not enjoy their conversation or their interests, but she could never envision being their wife. Those sorts of men were never willing to share. They wanted all the glory for themselves and would never listen to a woman's viewpoint—not really. They simply wanted someone who would not be utterly bored by their interest in history and wouldn't complain if they were gone for months on end. They saw what she did for her father and wanted it for themselves, but the difference was, she loved her father. She had certainly never loved any of them.

"I have little idea why you are so interested in me getting

a husband. Surely it is you who should be worrying about marriage? You have yet to sire an heir." She paused. "Or have you?"

He laughed, which turned into a coughing fit. Hannah patted him on his back until the fit ended. "Not at all. No children to my name," he said, his eyes watery. "Damned soup is trying to kill me," he muttered.

"I do not think you can rightly blame the soup. Now finish it up."

"Yes, milady. Whatever you say, milady."

She shook her head at the faux country accent and concentrated on her own morning meal of some coffee and a slice of bread slathered with honey. Red finished his soup before she had swallowed the last morsel and held out his empty bowl proudly.

"Are you proud of me, Hannah?"

She snatched the bowl off him. "What a ridiculous notion." And now she wished he was not using her name. It made the situation all the more intimate, as though she might be his wife nursing him. He certainly played the role of stubborn husband well. "Will you have the porridge too?"

He shook his head. "I'm not hungry." Red held up both palms. "And before you try to bully me into it, I am feeling a little revived, but I cannot stomach anymore food. If you want me to eat it, you'll have to force feed me."

"I do not think we have to go to those extremes." She placed the back of her hand to his forehead. He shuddered at the touch. "You are still warm. Perhaps I should see if there is an apothecary."

"I don't need any damned potions."

"Had anyone ever told you that you are a terrible patient?"

"Never." He stared up at her. "But no one has ever nursed me through sickness before. And you are a terrible nurse."

"I'm an excellent nurse." She lifted her chin. "You are making this much more difficult than it needs to be." She frowned. "Did your mother or your nursemaid never care for you while you were ill?"

"My mother died when my brother was born, and I was never sick. I'm as strong as an ox. Always have been."

"Well ox or not, you are not at all well. Stay in bed and sleep if you can. I shall inquire as to whether there is a local doctor or apothecary. At the very least, a tincture would help."

"As long as you do not bring someone here to let my blood, I'll take all the tinctures you want—much good they will do."

"I cannot fathom why you would think bloodletting might help, but I can promise you, I have no intention of letting that happen." She pulled on her bonnet and did up the ribbon.

"I've seen too many doctors turn to bloodletting as a treatment. Too many deaths from it too."

She nodded. "As have many, I'm sure." She offered a smile. "Trust me, Red. I do know what I am doing. I've nursed my father through illness, and he is a far more difficult patient than you."

"Oh." He raised his brows. "I shall have to try harder then."

Hannah chuckled as she left the room. That man could likely be on his deathbed and would still be trying to rile her.

She asked one of the serving maids about finding a physician and discovered there was indeed an apothecary, but the nearest doctor was five miles away. Red was not on his deathbed yet so she did not think they would have to send for anyone. She opted to visit the apothecary and came back with several tinctures that were promised to help, along with a salve for his chest to help his breathing.

When she returned to their room, Red was asleep, his snores as loud as ever. Sweat clung to his brow, and Hannah eyed him closely. His skin had taken on a pale cast that it had not held before. His skin was clammy but cool. Goodness, she hoped she had not misjudged it and he was sicker than either of them thought.

She remained at his bedside, damping him down as he heated up and covering him when he began to shiver. It was not until late afternoon that he finally stirred properly. He peered at her.

"Have you been there the whole time?"

"Yes."

"I thought you were. I could sense you. I'm glad you were." He tried to push up to sitting but quickly gave up.

"You are quite sick, Red. Rest, if you please."

He shook his head. "Never get sick." His words were almost mere puffs of air and she had to lean close to hear them.

"You are more sick than we thought," she said softly, not wishing to disturb him. "Will you take some tincture?"

"You're the boss of me, Hannah. Do with me what you will."

Had the circumstances been different, she could have thought of a few things to do with him. Throw him off a cliff...or kiss him. Either had run through her mind several times during their brief acquaintance.

She helped him take the tincture and unscrewed the lid of the salve. "This will help you breathe."

He eyed the yellowy goop as she put it on her finger. "I am not eating that."

Laughing, she pushed opened the neck of his shirt. True to his word, he let her do with him what she would, lying back and giving her full access. "This is for your chest. It will help you breathe better."

He closed his eyes and for that she was grateful. She did not want him watching her while she touched him so intimately. The hair on his chest was indeed soft—soft over hard muscle. What a contradiction he was.

Her skin heated while she spread the salve. A knot gathered in her throat. If she peered down, she could see the ridges of his stomach under his shirt. Red fell asleep while she tended to him, seeming to settle into a more peaceful rest.

Hannah took the chance to clean her hands and give herself some space from him. Though she could not help but sit on the chair and watch his profile and the rise and fall of his chest until supper time. It seemed that no matter how much she studied him, he would always take her by surprise. He had liked that she was here tending to him, remaining by his side. This dangerous smuggler had wanted her by his side during his sickness.

And she wanted to be here. What a mystery this all was. She pressed fingertips between her brows. History—and even the artifact—was easier to decipher than he was. Would she ever fully understand him?

CHAPTER FIFTEEN

Though Red's head thudded a little, he was certainly nowhere near as ill as he had been once they boarded the mail coach late on Thursday evening. They were the only travelers for which he was grateful as it meant he could spread his legs and get comfortable. A little achiness resided in his muscles and his voice was hoarse. However, Hannah's diligent care had meant he'd recovered well enough to continue their journey.

"Do you have the stone?" she asked, removing her bonnet and placing it on her lap.

"Of course. I'm not a fool."

"I was only checking. You have been very tired these past few days."

"It's there." He nudged the object with his foot.

"Good. Hopefully we shall make Plymouth by tomorrow evening."

"As long as no other disasters befall us."

"I am sure all will be well. You can hardly blame the stone for your illness. That was entirely your fault."

"Oh yes, I summoned the rains, did I not?"

"You could have taken the time to dry yourself or change your shirt, but you were too busy trying to be a man." She dropped her voice for the last part, imitating some kind of manly tone. He chuckled.

She laughed too, and the sound warmed him from the inside out.

"Well, I have learned my lesson though I shall admit, it was not all terrible being nursed back to health."

She lifted a brow. "Oh?"

The coach began to move, and she gripped the window ledge to prevent her from rocking forward. Red could not help putting out his arm and pinning her back against the seat until the motion had steadied.

Though it was growing late, the day had decided to bless them with a stunning sunset. Orange and pink streamed across the sky, broken up by a few thin lines of grey cloud. The colors lit the interior of the carriage, allowing him to look directly into Hannah's eyes. He held her gaze for a moment. Perhaps because he was unable to do anything else or perhaps because he simply enjoyed looking at her. It had become somewhat of a habit, observing her. Yes, he had done it throughout their acquaintance, but his sickness had taught him to look closer.

While he had been abed, she had begun copying the script from the stone. She would sit with her lips pursed, a tiny crinkle between her brows and lead stains on her fingers. If she touched her face, she left a mark, and he would long to reach forward and rub it off. Hannah St. John was more intriguing than he could have ever imagined.

He broke the look and settled back into the seat before he got himself in trouble.

"You were an excellent nurse," he said.

"Really? I do seem to recall you saying I was a terrible nurse."

He grinned. "You said I was a terrible patient."

"You were. You are. I stand entirely by those words." She straightened her back, but a smile teased her lips. "The worst patient I have ever nursed."

"Well, you may not have enjoyed nursing me, but I will not complain. You can be very tender, Hannah."

She peered out of the window at the sunset, seeming to take a moment to enjoy it. When she turned to eye him, the golden color skimmed her cheek, smoothing her features to a beautiful perfection.

"You seem surprised that I have a tender side."

"Not surprised." He flicked a curl out from behind her ear. "The light makes your hair shiny."

She batted his hand away. "Do not change the subject, Red. Do I seem so very heartless?"

"Not heartless as such but..."

"But?"

"You subscribe to logic."

"I do."

"In my experience, people like yourself—those who care mostly for intellectual pursuits—cannot summon up much empathy for the sick."

She shook her head. "You really do think me heartless."

"I never said such a thing, and besides, I knew from the beginning you were not or else you would not risk trekking across the country for your father."

"I wanted to ensure the stone was safe too."

"You cannot tell me you would do the same for just any man."

She pursed her lips. "I suppose not."

"See? Wrapped in that bluestocking exterior is a sweet, caring woman, and I am honored to have met her."

Hanna narrowed her eyes to slits at him. "If you think I

will take bluestocking as an insult, you are wrong. I am happy to be classed as one."

"I did not mean it as an insult." He sat back again, drawing his hat over his face. "If you will insist on taking everything I say the wrong way, I think I shall give up."

Her exasperated huff made him smile, but he managed to pinch it into a bored expression and close his eyes. Teasing her was far too much fun. He suspected they could go on for days. Hannah would never let herself be defeated. Better to let her stew for a little while before continuing.

He did indeed manage to drift off but awoke when they stopped to feed and water the horses. The night had taken over the sky and left it star speckled. He peered up at it out of the window and stared until he could see no single patch of black sky without spotting yet more stars.

Hannah stirred beside him. "Are we there yet?"

He smiled at her sleepy expression. "Not yet. Go back to sleep."

"It's a beautiful night," she mumbled before resting her head against his shoulder.

"Yes, it is," he agreed, watching her eyes close and face relax.

She slept, even as the horses were tethered and they started on their way again. As light from several cottage windows stole into the carriage, Red took the opportunity to study Hannah's relaxed expression. What a conundrum she was—all complex intellect and demanding courage combined with what he suspected was a bit of a silly sense of humor and a great deal of softness. Only a caring woman would go as far as she did for her father.

He contemplated this—and why it intrigued him—until he fell asleep, still none the wiser. When he next awoke, the scent of sea salt teased him awake, and he could hear the squawk of seagulls. He eased open one eye, then the other and bright light broke through his sleepiness. He grimaced. When he tried to move, his neck gave an almighty crack. Likely once he attempted to move the rest of him, every other joint would behave in a similar fashion.

He was bold enough to twist his head to view Hannah but winced as his muscles screamed in protest. Having been ill combined with sleeping on a chair designed for anything but had left him feeling about eighty.

She turned a smile toward him. "You're awake."

"I believe so," he grumbled.

"We are here, I believe."

He nodded and peered out at the passing scenery. The road was no longer lined with tufts of grass and the occasional rock and tree. Instead they passed fishermen's cottages on one side and a long, black railing on the other. The sea spanned to the horizon behind that railing, speckled with a few ships. Sunlight glinted off white tips that rolled with a little too much aggression for his liking. They were under a rare patch of sunshine. It looked as though direr weather was rolling in off the coast. He twisted his head to eye the clouds farther away and nodded to himself. A large grey band loomed aggressively, as though chasing them.

The carriage took them deeper into the cobbled streets of the town. The hour was early, but merchants and seamen were already awake, readying themselves to bring in and sell the catch of the day. Most of the cottages were painted white though some had shutters painted in more flamboyant colors —pink, blue, even a mint green. It was not dissimilar to home, but they were a mere hop across the estuary from Devon.

The mail coach came to a stop outside the mail house. Red had paid for their journey upfront so let the men get on with their duties and concentrated on ensuring Hannah and the stone were safely removed from the carriage. She tied her bonnet tight around her head and hefted her bag into her arms.

"You have the stone?"

"Of course."

"There is no need to be snappish," she scolded lightly. "You're not a morning person, are you, Red?"

He hefted the artifact into his arms. "Is anyone?"

"The morning can be a wonderful time. At home it is the most peaceful time of day. I prefer it for working."

Red snorted. "I prefer it for sleeping." He scowled at her. "For a well-bred lady, you certainly seem to enjoy working far too much. Why do you not take a moment to enjoy a rest or whatever it is that young ladies do to relax?"

She gave him a sour look. "You know very well what young ladies do. They embroider or play piano or share gossip with their friends."

"And you would rather bury yourself in the history books or stare at some old, dusty object," he finished for her.

"Precisely." She beamed.

He nodded down a tightly wound alley. "The driver said the ferryman is down this way."

Hannah strode ahead, affording him a view of her from behind. There was something oddly enticing about her funny little walk. She moved with purpose, but not being tall, she could hardly take the biggest steps. It was a walk designed for the simplest of purposes—to move from point *a* to point *b*—with little thought as to what anyone watching might think. There was no subtle sway of her hips or delicate arch of her back. He had to admit, he rather liked that. She was quite adorable and utterly clueless to it, and thus, became even more adorable.

He sighed to himself as they emerged from between the buildings and out onto the harbor side. If his friends could hear his thoughts...well, they would think he was due a stay at the lunatic asylum. Adorable, honestly. What sort of an earl-turned-smuggler even uttered such words let alone dwelled on it?

Red took another glance at the sky and then at the great distance the boat would have to cover to get to the other side. On a fine day, he would have no concerns, but the tide was high and the water had already become choppy.

"Hannah," he called, stopping her before she reached the sign that had been awkwardly chalked with 'Ferri'. "We may have to consider going around."

An old man, and most certainly an ex-fisherman, eased himself up from his position on one of the wooden poles that lined the harbor side. He moved with all the stiffness of a man with the sea in his joints. A tuft of white hair flared from beneath a worn cap, and when he smiled, he was all gums and a few yellow teeth.

"You want the ferry?"

Hannah nodded. "Yes, please."

Red closed the distance and took a step in front of Hannah. "The weather is coming in."

The old man made a dismissive sound. "I have gone through far worse and in a boat that was only suitable for driftwood. I'll get you to the other side. If you can pay, that is."

"Of course we can," Hannah said.

Red's gut tightened. He didn't like the look of this one bit. "The crossing is getting choppy."

The fisherman straightened, releasing a crack that made Red's early body woes seem like nothing. "Now see here, sonny, I've got more experience of the sea in my finger than you have in your entire body."

Red tugged Hannah aside and leaned in. "I have a bad feeling about this."

She eyed him, one brow lifted. "If he thinks all is well, I

would be more inclined to believe him. I am sure he has no desire to drown any more than we do."

Jaw tight, he shook his head. "We should go around. I'll arrange a carriage."

"And how much time will that add onto our journey?"

He considered the distance to the nearest bridge. "A day and a half."

"We cannot have any more delays. I must get this to London. Think logically, Red. Why would this man risk death for a few coin?"

"I think this old man doesn't care what he's risking. He's not far off his deathbed anyway," he hissed. "I am telling you, Hannah, I have a bad feeling about this."

She ran her gaze up and down him. "Quite frankly, logic trumps your gut feeling. We must take the ferry."

"And if I choose not to?"

"I will go without you. I shall find someone on the other side willing to carry the stone, I'm sure. You are no longer the only physically capable man around, and no one here believes in any silly kind of curse."

Red pinched the bridge of his nose. Was he really going to risk drowning for this irritating woman and her bloody stone?

Apparently yes.

"Fine, have it your way. But I shall haunt you in the after-life if I drown."

"We shall be fine." She smiled at the fishermen. "We would like you to take us across please."

The old man unpeeled one bony hand. "Payment up front."

"In case we drown and he does not," Red grumbled to Hannah.

She nudged him with an elbow, and Red paid the man. Red aided Hannah into the unsteady boat and flung down his bag to her. She caught it with an *oof* and narrowed her gaze at him.

He smiled innocently. "Careful. Don't want my belongings going overboard. An earl cannot wander around naked, you know. It is not good manners."

"I was not going to drop it, but you might have thrown it more gently."

He stepped in awkwardly, terribly aware that if he or his luggage fell in, Hannah would not be bothered one jot, but if the stone went in, there would be hell to pay. He cradled it close as he settled on the bench opposite her with his back to the fisherman.

The vessel rocked unsteadily while the old man positioned himself and lifted the oars. They were crossing at one of the smaller parts of the estuary, but it was still at least a half an hour boat ride by his reckoning—perhaps more if the state of their captain was anything to go by.

Waves rolled under them, making each minute of the journey a heart-wrenching experience. He focused on the other side and willed it to draw closer whilst keeping an eye on the clouds above, the steel band of grey invading ever closer. The first raindrop made his stomach tighten. The sudden gust of one hundred more had him gripping onto the side of the boat.

"Seen worse," the fisherman shouted over the heavy din of drops on wood.

Red turned his attention to Hannah, whose fingers were curled just as tightly around the seat beneath her. Her gaze reluctantly locked with his, and he saw her fear there. Had he not felt the same, he might have taken a little delight in the fact that there was also an unspoken message there. Perhaps, just perhaps—because Hannah would never admit these things with ease—he was right.

He longed to take her into his arms and hold her tight,

but he dare not move for fear of destabilizing the boat. He was powerless to do anything but hold on and pray that the boat did not tip and Hannah did not go overboard. If she did, he would go in without hesitation, but he doubted either of them would survive. The murky green sea would swallow them whole.

Swiping the raindrops from his face, he focused on the other side. A glimmer of sunlight still lit a strip across the beach that awaited them. The grey harbor wall was set back from the long stretch of sand and farther still were all the cottages. Everything seemed too far away.

A wave hit them, rocking the boat and its contents to one side. Hannah screamed. Red darted forward and thrust forward an arm to prevent her spilling into the water. The boat shifted back, sending their bags rolling. Before Red could prevent it, Hannah's bag seemed to take a suicidal leap into the water. He snatched for it but it was too late. The sea gulped it down, leaving no sign of it.

Neither of them could do anything but sit and hold on tight while further swells rocked the boat, each one threatening to tip more than their luggage into the sea. The rain soaked under Red's collar, and he had no doubt Hannah was wet to her chemise. Inside the boat, the wood was wet and slippery—perfect for sending them all to their doom. For several more minutes, the old man battled them through until the rain eased away to droplets and then vanished.

The sea clung to its anger for a little longer until the estuary grew shallower. Red finally released his death grip on the boat and reached over for Hannah. She grasped his hand gratefully, no doubt aware of how close to death they had been.

Relief coursed through him when the boat hit sand. The old man jumped out, and Red followed him, keen to get them to shore as quickly as possible. His boots protected him from most of the water though some sloshed over the edges as they hauled the boat up the sand.

"Told you I'd seen worse," the man said, cracking a grin.

Red somehow did not unleash the torrent of words that were burning inside him on the old man. At least they were here, in one piece, and alive.

Red grabbed the stone and his bag, mindful of the fact they were one bag lighter. Hannah kept her head lowered, but he saw her bottom lip drawn under teeth and he heard her sniffle. The torrent of rain had eased to a patter, but her bonnet was a wilting mess. They trudged up the beach to the harbor wall and climbed the stone steps. He grimaced when he spotted her shaking shoulders. She was likely frozen through.

"W-where are we headed now?"

She wasn't cold. Well, she likely was, but that was not causing the shaking shoulders. He heard the tremor in her voice and understood it well enough.

He took her shoulders in his hands. "Hannah?"

She kept her face lowered, but a sob broke her. He pressed her hard to his chest and another sob bubbled from her. Her cold body shook against his, and he rubbed a hand up and down her back.

"W-we nearly drowned," she spluttered out. "It would have been all my fault. We could have died. H-how could I have been so stupid?"

"I should never have given in. I knew it was dangerous. I'm meant to protect you. It was my fault, Hannah."

She peered up at him and drew in a long sniffle. He smoothed the damp curls from her cheeks and held her face in his hands. "I left you with no choice, I know that. I'm so stupid and stubborn and..."

"Enough."

He brought his mouth down on hers. She squeaked and

fell silent. He was so absurdly grateful for the warm taste of her, for the knowledge that they had both survived. He had gone through many a heart-stopping moment what with the excise men and a dangerous profession but never had he really thought himself close to death. Worse was the idea that he might have lost Hannah.

She softened into him like butter melting in the sun. Her hips bumped into his, her breasts pressed against his chest. He pushed the kiss deeper and held her firm against him with his palms either side of her head. Her hands swept up his back. He kissed her until he felt warm and alive again, and then kissed her some more. When he drew back, the tears had vanished and a warm flush was on her cheeks.

"We both made a mistake there," he told her. "But I should never have agreed to do it. I should have flung you over my shoulder and taken you to the nearest carriage for hire."

"I am sorry," she said, tucking one plump lip beneath her teeth again.

"No apologies."

She nodded. "What now?"

"Let us find an inn where we can warm by the fire and have some food. Then I shall inquire about a carriage."

She held out a hand to his bag. "Shall I carry that? Seeing as I have nothing to carry now."

He shook his head. "Do I look like I need a woman to carry my belongings?"

"I was just..." A vulnerable look swept across her face again. He supposed she was so damned used to always being right, it had to be hard to have made the wrong decision. But what he'd said was true. He should never have given in to her. He'd been too weak and foolish. Hannah had quite the ability to beat down his defenses. He would have to be more careful from now on.

"Was there anything valuable in your bag?"

"Not really. A little bit of jewelry, but I do not travel with valuables. I regret losing my blue muslin though. And I certainly regret having only one dress for the rest of the journey."

Red had already considered how they would sort out a new wardrobe for her. This town would have a dressmaker, but there would be no chance they could put together something quickly enough. They would stop in Exeter shortly—a much bigger town. Perhaps they could find something there.

"Come, let us find some food and warmth." He could not bear her standing about shivering like a little girl who had just lost her stuffed toy.

She nodded, mournfully glancing at the sea that had swallowed her belongings. The stone tucked under his arm seemed to grow heavier. Never in his life had he experienced such bad luck. He could not wait to be rid of the blasted thing.

Still, he was not sure he could say the same about Hannah.

CHAPTER SIXTEEN

It was a fine thing the Fir Tree had a roaring fire going considering Hannah had no change of clothes. Mortification still stung her cheeks even as she dried in their position by the fire. The inn was not much different to the Ship with its clouded windows and low beamed roof. They sat, tucked in one corner, with the fire giving off a welcoming warmth. After a generous sized pork pie and a helping of brandy that Red had insisted on, she was feeling almost human.

But still embarrassed.

What a fool she had been. Why had she been so stubborn? Why must she always insist on doing things her way? She had been an unbearable burden on this journey, dragging Red into her mess, even though he had wanted nothing to do with her. How arrogantly she had behaved, believing they could somehow defeat nature. Well, she would not make that mistake again. Was research not about studying everything and coming to a conclusion rather than blindly blundering along with one's own conclusion? Clearly, she had not learned as much as she had thought from her father. She should have listened to Red.

He stood at the bar now, conversing with the barkeep, likely trying to find out about transport to Taunton. She was happy to let him take charge after her blundering. She would only make a big mess of it and probably have them on a carriage that would take them all the way back to Land's End or something.

"Enough sulking," Red said as he strode back over.

She lifted her gaze from the empty brandy glass and let her attention roll over the long length off him. He'd abandoned his greatcoat to the back of his chair to let it dry, and his jacket was open, revealing his waistcoat. She followed each golden button up to his cravat and then traced the shadowed stubble on his jaw. It had felt rough against her skin but not unpleasant.

The kiss seemed a blur now. Entirely natural and needed, and yet it had happened in a mere moment and ended all too soon. All she had known was she was grateful to be alive and needed to feel his lips upon hers. It was a trifle inconvenient wanting to kiss him all the time—and not at all ladylike. What would her father think of her?

She laughed to herself. He would likely not even notice if she kissed Red right in front of him. Her father had never paid much attention to her minimal courting life. He was too busy studying.

"I am not sulking," she finally said.

No, she was just mightily ashamed of herself. She would try to be better, though. She would prove to him that she could listen to him and take on board his opinion—that she was not some demanding harpy who always thought herself right.

"A stagecoach goes from the market square." He pulled out his pocket watch. "We only have half an hour before it leaves. It will take us to Exeter."

She nodded. "That's good."

She followed him out of the inn, feeling very much like the meek and mild little lady, following after the man in charge. And it was better that way. Men liked their women quiet and for good reason. Hannah bet meek and mild women never nearly drowned anyone.

They followed the harbor wall to the town square. The tide had come in further and several boys were fishing, using rods made from sticks and string and a few worms as bait. A cry came from one of them, making Hannah pause and press a hand to her chest.

"What is it?" one of the boys asked, racing over to his friend's side.

The lad who had cried out drew out a white garment with a flourish. "It's a corset!" he declared, glee written on his face.

All the other boys gathered around and began fingering the sodden cotton and lace. Hannah cringed.

"Should I rescue it from them?" Red did a poor job of hiding his amusement as he pressed his lips together.

She shook her head. "It is ruined now, and I certainly have no wish to claim it."

They moved on toward the cobbled square which was centered around a memorial to men lost at sea. "I suppose you think I got what I deserved," she said quietly as she studied the names and ages carved into the stone plinth.

"Hannah, if you think I wished you to learn a lesson by nearly drowning, you are sorely wrong. However, it is a little amusing."

"For you perhaps. You did not have young boys playing with your undergarments."

"Think of the joy you brought them."

"I would rather not."

"If it is any consolation, I nearly drowned myself when I first began, uh, my extra activities."

She turned to face him, trying to imagine this strong man overcome by waves. "How?"

"I misjudged the depth of the water when bringing in some goods. It was the early days, and as much as I might have lived by the sea all my life, I am no seaman." He motioned out toward the beach. "Drake deposits them on the ocean bed, ensuring they're weighted down. The goods are hidden from sight and can be collected by night."

"That sounds dangerous."

He smirked. "Smuggling *is* dangerous."

She glanced around, fearful someone might overhear but the square was not too busy with only a few people strolling through. "So you go into the sea to collect them."

"Yes. They're at a depth where you can get them easily enough, but it has to be deep enough so the excise men do not spot them. If the sea is a bit rough it is not usually a problem, but we had not figured out the best point to deposit them yet. It was early days for us, you understand."

She nodded. Well, she understood what he meant but the whole smuggling thing was hard to understand. Why did he take such risks?

"It was out of my depth and the weather was poor. A freak wave grabbed me and pulled me under. Were it not for Knight, I would have drowned. Thankfully he's the size of a house or else we would have both gone under." He shook his head and gave a half smile. "I should have listened to my gut and left it until the waves had calmed. Needless to say, I understand the water a little better these days."

"So you always listen to your gut now?"

"Always."

She considered her own stomach and did not feel anything in it apart from being full from the meal. "I am not sure I have a 'gut instinct.'"

"Perhaps you are too busy trying to think logically to listen to your gut."

Hannah frowned but was saved from defending herself by the interruption of a short, well-dressed gentleman.

"I say, are you waiting for the stage?"

Hannah glanced over him. His round cheeks were lined with great slashes of hair that ran all the way down his jawline. His cheeks were ruddy and his nose was bulbous and a similar hue. He wore a rigid top hat and buckskins. Beside him, a female companion of similar age offered the same open expression—a wide smile on her face. She could have been his sister, sporting the same rounded figure with a generous bust and rosy cheeks. Her grey hair was curled carefully and topped with a wide-brimmed bonnet. She wore a fine gown of silk and lace.

"Yes, indeed we are," Red replied.

"You're the earl, are you not? the man asked, his eyes wide with excitement.

"I suppose so." Red's voice was edged with hesitation.

"See, dear. We are to share a stage with an earl. Is that not wonderful? Did I not tell you this would be a fine journey indeed? And there you were fretting about the weather."

"Oh you tease." The woman smacked his arm lightly. "I was not fretting at all. I merely said the weather looked a little grim. I am hardly the sort to be afraid of a little rain."

"Oh no indeed. No woman is ever afraid of a little rain ruining their hair or bonnet." He winked at Red, who appeared utterly baffled by the overly talkative couple. "Now will you complain at me for making us wait a day to travel? I do not think you will, will you, my dear? Not when we have fine company with us." The man finally drew breath. "I am Lord Crawford and this charming creature who does so loathe the rain is my wife, Lady Crawford."

"A pleasure," Red said, with some hesitation. "Lord

Redmere, at your service. And this is my cousin Miss
St. John."

The words tripped off his tongue so easily, Hannah
almost startled at them. Of course they had been travelling
under the guise of some family relation, but she had never
actually heard him say the words. She only hoped these
people did not press for more information as to how exactly
they were related. Hannah had travelled plenty on her own
but never in the company of a man who was not her family.
Scandal would hardly follow her—she was not really important enough for such things—but she would not wish to
cause any gossip.

"See, my dear?" Lord Crawford said, nudging his wife.
"We are travelling in fine company. Are you not glad I took
the lead and decided we should leave today?"

His wife released a wide smile. "I am indeed. Goodness
knows we are in want of good company. Plymouth is a
pleasant sort of town, but there is no one to visit with. I am
practically ravenous for some fine company and even better
gossip. Tell me, where did you travel from? Redmere?"

Red hardly seemed to know what to do with the chatty
couple. His arrogant facade had come across his face and his
lips were tightly pinched. She could practically feel the dread
coming off him. He had no inclination whatsoever to spend a
day travelling with them. However, they had little choice and
at least the couple were pleasant, if a little gauche.

Hannah smiled. "Yes—at least nearby."

"So you have had quite a journey already," Lord Crawford
concluded. "And where do you travel to? We have been
visiting with my lady wife's dear sister and her seven
children."

"Oh you silly bean, she has nine," his wife corrected.

"Oh goodness." The man chuckled. "Nine! Who on earth
could keep up? Every time I tried to count, they moved and I

had to start again." He drew out his pocket watch and gave it a quick glance. "Anyway, we have been—Ah, here comes our transport."

Hannah practically heard Red's long exhale. She pressed a warning hand to his arm. They needed this coach if they were to progress to Exeter, and she did not much want him to be rude to their travelling companions. For an earl, he really did lack airs and graces sometimes. She smiled as he grumbled something under his breath. She supposed she could not complain about that. There was nothing false about Red, and there was something refreshing about that.

Their belongings were loaded onto the chaise, and Red handed Hannah into the coach before sitting beside her. The vehicle, drawn by four horses, was a little finer than the mail coach with a plush velvet interior and comfortable cushions. Hannah's weary body accepted the comfort of them with ease. Sleeping in a mail coach really did nothing for one's muscles.

Lady Crawford beamed at Hannah. "Are you stopping at Exeter?"

Hannah shook her head. "We are to travel on to London. We hope to hire a private coach."

Lord Crawford gave her a sympathetic look. "Are you from London, my dear? No doubt you find the travelling in Cornwall and Devon most barbaric, having to stop all the time and cross these pesky rivers."

She tried not to think about their river crossing earlier today and her undergarments hanging from a boy's fishing rod. No doubt it would one day be a tale to amuse, but at present, it brought her more shame than enjoyment.

"I reside in Hampshire, but I visit London on a regular basis. The transport is certainly not quite so...organized as in London."

Lady Crawford chuckled. "You are a diplomatic young

woman. Travelling in Devon is quite a to do as myself and my husband are aware. I adore visiting with my sister—"

"She adores doting on all her eleven children," her husband interrupted.

"Oh you tease." She tapped his leg.

"You know she has nine."

"And you cannot resist spoiling a single one of them."

"That I cannot," she confided in Hannah. "However, I do tire of the journey, even though it is but two days. I cannot imagine how you feel about your journey ahead. No doubt you are weary already."

"Yes, weary indeed," Red drawled.

If the woman had heard the hint there, she showed no sign of it. "Well, we shall have a jolly good journey and hopefully provide you with a little break from the tedium of travelling. I imagine you are much better at travelling than us, Miss St. John, but we shall try our best to rise to the challenge."

Hannah saw Red's jaw ticking. She surreptitiously gave his arm a reassuring squeeze. They would only be travelling with the couple for two days. It could hardly be any worse than what they had already experienced so far.

The woman continued on much the same vein until they reached the coaching inn. Her husband was a viscount, they discovered, with a sizeable estate in Devon.

Her husband interjected at most moments and delighted in teasing his wife. Never had Hannah witnessed such frivolity and humor. If she were not so tired, she might have been more amused, but by the time they had climbed stiffly up to their bed, their stomachs full with generous pork cutlets, she had quite the headache. Red shut the door to their room and pressed his back to it.

"If I heard another word from her, I was likely to stuff my cravat in her mouth."

"That is not very gentlemanly." She tugged off her gloves and put them on the side. She grimaced at her creased dress. What would they think of her, wearing the same gown tomorrow? She shook her head at herself. Whatever they thought, it was her fault and she would have to suffer the consequences of her foolish decision.

"I am not always very gentlemanly," Red said, casting his gaze over her.

The breath in her lungs froze. Her lips parted of their own accord.

His eyes were dark, some secret message written in them, and she longed to find out what it was. Even after a day of travelling, he pulled at something inside her. Something that willed her to throw herself against him and feel every part of that strong body with absolute leisure. With his chestnut hair slightly wild and his cravat pulled loose, he was every inch the roguish lord. She had never thought herself intrigued by such men—but then, she had never met Red before.

"Get some sleep," he said softly.

The words jolted her. She frowned.

"Get some sleep, Hannah. We have a long day ahead, and I am tired. I have no wish to do something we will both regret."

Hannah almost wished he had not said that as she tucked herself in under the blankets. What would they both regret? A kiss? Something more? Did he...did he wish to make love to her? She could not be sure, after all, no man had ever revealed such a wish to her before, but if she analyzed it carefully...

CHAPTER SEVENTEEN

The viscount and viscountess were in high spirits the next morning. Red's insides shriveled a little as they greeted them brightly. Red ensured he spent as much time as possible overseeing the loading of the luggage and the damned stone before joining them inside the carriage.

"You are a good man, my lord, making sure we are all set to go. Did you sleep well?" Lady Crawford asked. "I tell you, I have only stayed in a few coaching inns, but that was quite a pleasant one indeed. Soft beds, do you not think?"

"Oh soft indeed," her husband put in. "Of course, I barely took a moment to enjoy it. I was fast asleep within moments, but that is what travelling does to you, is it not?"

"Of course Miss St. John would know better than us, would she not, my dear? She is a regular traveler." The viscountess smiled.

Hannah tried to protest. "Oh I do not know about—"

"I knew you were asleep within an instant, George, as your snores were rattling the eaves." Lady Crawford laughed and gripped the window ledge when the carriage began to move. "I am surprised the whole inn did not hear it. I hope my husband did not keep you awake. I will confess I am used to it so I sleep straight through it."

"Why, it is almost like a lullaby to her!" the viscount declared. "I think if I stopped you would not sleep a wink, my dear."

They both laughed. "You are quite right," she agreed. "What a state of affairs it is when you need a snoring man to soothe you to sleep."

Hannah offered a polite smile.

"You found the accommodations acceptable?" Lord Crawford pressed Red.

"Quite acceptable," he said through a tight jaw.

Hannah had insisted that they were lucky to have such nice travelling companions—and indeed they were certainly not rude or arrogant, but how anyone could talk as much as they did about absolutely nothing, he had no idea. Perhaps in other circumstances he might have found them amusing or at least tolerable, but after another sleepless night—one in which he was consumed by wild thoughts of Hannah—he had little patience for them.

Hannah kept giving him little touches or squeezes, mostly to prevent him from saying something uncouth, he suspected, but she could have no idea that they were gradually driving him closer to the edge of lunacy.

That kiss had been a mistake and one that neither of them had been able to resist. Hannah had not mentioned it, and he didn't believe she regretted it. They had both simply been grateful to be alive and had expressed it with that kiss. There had been nothing more natural at the time.

Last night, however...if he had kissed her then, it would have been a choice. Then he would have chosen to take it further. He would have opted to touch her, to skim a hand under her garments and feel her smooth skin. He would have desired to see her eyelids flutter when he touched her higher or deeper. Were it not for the remembrance that she was utterly inexperienced, he might well have gone ahead and done that. Perhaps she would have let him too. He had seen that want there, deep in her eyes.

Red opted for fixing his attention on the view when he could. The viscount and viscountess demanded his attention at times but eventually fell into talking between themselves. Not that is was the hushed sort of conversation that allowed other occupants to talk amongst themselves, but at least they no longer required his participation.

They stopped to change horses and eat, which seemed to revive the couple. Red wished he could say the same. A heavy weight filled his gut at the idea of remaining in a closed space with them.

"Be polite," Hannah reminded him. "We only have one more afternoon of travelling. Perhaps if you engaged them in conversation you would find it easier."

"Are you giving me life lessons?" he grumbled.

"They are nice people. The journey passed more quickly when I talked to them. If you listen carefully, you will find they are interesting people."

He shook his head. "Of course you can find interest in them, Hannah. You can find interest in a bloody rock."

She rolled her eyes at him. "And you cannot find anything good in anything. You are nothing more than a jaded, grumpy old smuggler."

"Oh I can find good," he declared. "I can find plenty of good. In fact, I would declare myself an expert in it." After all, he had found something insanely desirable about this frustrating bluestocking in front of him.

"Really? Prove it."

"Prove what?"

"That you are not really a miserable old man. Find something you like about these people."

He was a grown man. He'd met many challenges and won them. He was certainly past betting or trying to prove herself. However, Hannah was smiling properly for the first time since their incident. She was feeling foolish, he knew that much, and likely a little scared still. If he could keep that smile on her face, he would play her game.

"Very well. I shall be the epitome of wit and charm for the rest of the journey. Let us see what is so wonderful about these people. I suspect by the end of this journey I shall be looking for a rope with which to hang myself."

"Do not be so dramatic," she scolded lightly.

As promised, Red laid on the charm for the rest of their travels. He flirted with the viscountess and engaged Lord Crawford in conversation of fishing and hunting as well as talk of looking after tenants. Hannah watched him for most of it, remaining relatively quiet but with a slight smile tilting her lips.

"What a shame we cannot travel farther together more," the viscount declared as they came into the town. "I believe we could learn a thing or two from each other, my lord."

Hannah was going to adore the fact that underneath all his bluster and talk, the viscount was a savvy investor as well as an intelligent man with a great deal of knowledge about new farming techniques. Red suspected there was little he could teach the man unless he wanted to be a smuggler.

"We must travel on to Taunton tomorrow. My hope is to arrange a private carriage."

"And why are you not travelling in yours now?" the viscountess asked.

Hannah chuckled. "We had somewhat of a disaster with the earl's carriage."

Red nodded. "We have had a mighty run of bad luck on this journey."

They both cast a glance at the stone that laid wrapped at their feet.

"Our sons and daughters are at home so we left the carriage with them," Lady Crawford confided. "They do so love to get out and about. You know how young people are...Well, of course you do." She laughed. "You are young people!"

"Dear wife, you are forgetful," Lord Crawford teased.

"I shall not forget that remark," she shot back with a grin.

"Oh dear, now I shall be in trouble when we are alone. Pray for me will you?"

Hannah beamed at them, somehow delighting in their incessant talk. At least they made her happy, he supposed, though he would have rather have passed the journey in silence. Or perhaps just in Hannah's company...

"You are a naughty man." His wife tutted. "Making me out to be so dreadfully awful."

"I don't need to do such a thing. They know it well." The viscount winked at Hannah.

"Oh no," protested Hannah.

Lady Crawford leaned forward, her hands clasped in her lap. "Anyway, as I was saying before my husband so rudely interrupted...we opted for the stage to take us to my sisters. Thankfully we did not have as great a journey as you two young folk. Our carriage is to meet us here tomorrow and take us home. Though I must say, I have been quite impressed with the service. I think we shall do it more often."

The viscount shook his head hastily. "We do not need to see your sister and her dozen children again anytime soon. My pocketbook says so."

"It is *nine* children." Lady Crawford rolled her eyes. "And your pocketbook can always stretch to treat them as you well know."

"Yes, but my back cannot take anymore jostling around in

a carriage. I imagine you two are mightily looking forward to your own beds."

"Indeed," Hannah said.

The carriage drew to a halt, having passed under the archway into the inn. When Red stepped out and ensured their belongings were all together, he shook the viscount's hand.

"Excellent company, my lord. I appreciate it. You know well enough how it can be travelling with women. All they do is talk."

Red somehow managed not to laugh. "Likewise, Crawford. You have given me a lot to think on."

Crawford's wife tugged on his arm. "Come now, let us get some food and away to bed. We are all tired and hungry, are we not? And I am sure Miss St. John is as fed up with talk of farming and hunting as I am."

Hannah and he dined separately from the couple due to the larger tables being occupied. There was no private dining room, but Red was not overly fussed. All he wanted was food, drink, and a nice bit of peace and quiet. The inn was unfortunately one of the more popular coaching inns, being on the road between Plymouth and Taunton, it hosted travelers going both ways as well as those heading north from the south coast. The generous building had three floors with rooms taking up both the top floors. Their room was on the middle one, facing out onto the busy street in front. He hoped it was not noisy tonight.

Hannah eyed him as he took a long gulp of ale.

"What is it?" he asked, lowering his tankard.

"You liked them."

"Liked is a strong word."

"Very well. You respected him at least."

"He is an informed man with some interesting ideas, I shall give you that." He narrowed his gaze at her. "There is no need to look so smug. Yes, I managed to find something with which to converse with them about, but I still found them to be the most irritating of people."

"I thought they were quite lovely, though I will confess I am looking forward to some peace."

"I had better not utter another word then."

"That is not what I meant!"

"Ah, so is the saintly Miss Hannah St. John admitting they were too much for her?"

"They are nice people, but goodness, they can talk. I'm not sure how they do it."

He peered their way. Several tables divided them and they could not hear what they were saying, but the Viscount lifted a beer in salute. Red returned the salute.

"Well, tomorrow we shall be on our way to Taunton, and if we can hire a private coach from there, we might only have four days of travelling left."

Four days. Four more days in Hannah's company. How was it he had begun to enjoy sitting with her for dinner, watching her smile or even frown as she contemplated something? How was it he liked her arguing with him, tell him how very wrong he always was?

Four days did not seem enough.

CHAPTER EIGHTEEN

Hannah was finishing her hair when Red re-entered the room. The habit of him vanishing while she readied herself for the day had become rather like the routine of a married couple, though today he had reason to vanish—he had been hunting out transport for them.

She glanced at him in the mirror. "Any luck?"

He shook his head. "I swear there is not a carriage in this whole damned town for hire." He tugged off his hat and laid it on the bed to push a hand through his hair. "The nearest mail coach goes from Taunton—the very place we need to be. Everything goes from bloody Taunton."

Hannah pushed a clip into her hair. She might have few belongings, but at least she had come away with enough grips in her hair to ensure that could be neat for the rest of their journey. As for her dress...well she was fast looking as though she had been living in the gutter. It was relatively stain-free, but there were a few mud splotches on the hem and creases from how she had been sitting on the coach. She grimaced at her reflection.

"We could walk?"

"It would take two days, and who knows if there is an inn on the way."

"Perhaps—oh." She paused and tugged her hand. She twisted to eye her reflection and saw her glove had become caught in her hair by one of the buttons. Trying to wriggle it free, she winced as her hair pulled.

"Is there a problem?"

His smug expression made her lift her chin and reply *no*. Red did so delight in her frustrations at times. She twisted her wrist and pulled again. "Damnation," she muttered under her breath.

"Such language."

She narrowed her gaze at him. "Will you help me please?"

He came closer and tilted his head to view the disaster she had tangled herself up in. Literally. "I quite like you like this. At least you cannot slap me."

"I have a free hand," she warned him. "Anyway, why would I slap you?"

He smirked at her in the mirror. "If you cannot imagine why, I will not say a word." He grasped her wrist. "Keep still," Red ordered.

Hannah obeyed and waited while he carefully released the button from the tangle of curls. He smoothed out her hair and put both arms around her to take her gloved wrist in his hands. Her gaze met his in the reflection. The position could hardly be more intimate. Her back was to his chest, her bottom nestled against his—

Anyway, his arms enveloped her and his face was beside hers. He tweaked the button that had become caught and did it up once more.

His gaze lifted back to hers, and he kept hold of her wrist in one hand. The other came to the side of her face and pushed aside the mess that was now her hair. His breath whispered across her ear, making her tremble.

"What are you doing?" she whispered.

"I wish I knew."

He pressed a kiss to just beneath her ear. The kiss was light, so feather-light. It should not have felt like anything but the brief touch of lips, but it sent tingles racing through her, and her entire body flamed in an instant.

"You're too damned beautiful, Hannah," Red said before releasing her.

She gaped at her reflection. How could he kiss her and say something like that then just release her?

He snatched up his hat. "I'm going to make some more inquiries."

Hannah had been unable to move until he shut the door. The latch clinking into place jolted her from the dreamlike state in which she'd found herself. She lifted fingers to her neck and touched her skin, still tingling from his kiss.

She was too beautiful? She eyed herself in the mirror. At present, she was a mess. Her hair was wild, her gown creased. Underneath that, perhaps she was pretty, but beautiful? No.

More puzzling was the fact he had admitted he did not know what he was doing when he embraced her. Red seemed like the sort of man who always knew what he was doing and when he was doing it. That he had even confessed as much to her made her soften to him. Some small part of him was unsure of himself and seeing that vulnerability made her want to know more. What else was under that arrogant, confident exterior? Those were elements of him to be certain, but she needed to find out more. The Earl of Redmere called for much closer study. She had four days at least, maybe more. Surely someone like herself could figure him out by then?

Finishing her hair, she pulled on her bonnet and put on her pelisse which covered the worst of the muck on her dress. It looked to be a relatively cool day but at least it was dry. If they were to walk, she wanted to be prepared.

Red was not in the inn so she stepped out into the courtyard only to be accosted by Lady Crawford.

"I have wonderful, wonderful news," the woman declared, motioning frantically to her husband, who was speaking with the driver of what had to be their private carriage.

"Oh yes?"

"Wonderful news," the viscountess repeated. "We have decided to add a few days to our excursion. I have a cousin in Taunton, and we are going to visit with her."

"Oh that's..." Hannah frowned, unsure what the woman expected of her.

"Well, we are going to give you and the earl a ride to Taunton, silly girl. Is that not wonderful?"

Hannah blinked. "Oh you really should not..."

The viscount strode over, his wide form bumbling across the courtyard. "I take it my dear wife has informed you we are to be travelling partners once more." He grinned widely. "One of the stable hands said you were struggling to find transport, and, well, we have transport and are not indisposed to extending our little break away from home, so we thought why not? I will confess it was my wife's idea, however, so I must not take credit."

"Oh, Lord Crawford, you suggested as much last night before we even knew of the transport troubles."

His ruddy cheeks reddened. "You did put the idea of visiting Taunton in my head, that I will admit. I only commented to my wife that it was a shame we could not continue our travels with you delightful young people. I have not enjoyed a jaunt across the country so much in a long time."

Hannah peered around for Red. "I am flattered indeed, I—"

"You get yourself ready and find that dashing earl. We shall be waiting," Lady Crawford insisted.

"Of course. We shall not be long." Hannah dashed away and paused. "Thank you."

She hastened out of the courtyard and studied the street in front of the inn. Where was he? He must be going to great lengths to secure some transport. She finally spotted him striding up the street, his gait determined but clearly frustrated.

"No luck?"

He shook his head. "I swear there is not even a farmer's cart to take us onward. This place is stuck in the medieval times." He scowled. "No, earlier than that. At least they had carriages and those boxes for hefting people about."

"I have some good news," she spilled out. "The Viscount and Viscountess Crawford have offered to take us on to Taunton."

Red stilled. "The Crawfords?"

"Indeed. They adore us so much that they have decided to visit some relations in Taunton and take us with them."

"Those Crawfords seem to have relations everywhere. I should make a note so I can begin avoiding all these places."

Hannah chuckled. It was true. Not only did Lady Crawford have many, many nieces and nephews, they had both related tales of family members across the breadth of England. Their family was prolific in numbers.

"They are waiting for us," she prompted. "We ought to hurry."

Face grim, he glanced up and down the street as though some other solution would prevent itself.

"This is our only opportunity, Red." She curled her fingers around his arm. "I just know it."

An eyebrow lifted at her declaration. "A carriage will turn up eventually. This is a damned coaching inn, after all."

She shook her head. "Eventually, but how long will we have to wait? This is our only chance, I'm sure of it."

"Your gut is speaking to you?"

Lifting a shoulder, she smiled. "Perhaps. But logically we cannot sit around when there is perfectly good transport out there, regardless of how much you loathe the company."

"I shall have trouble being polite for much longer," he grumbled. "The chances are I shall be rude, and they shall kick us out of the carriage on our arses."

"I do not think that's a possibility. Apparently they think we are simply wonderful and what we have done to deserve such accolades, I cannot tell you, but there we have it."

He hefted in a breath and released it slowly, giving the empty street one longing look, likely hoping a carriage travelling directly to Taunton would appear.

"Come on then, let us get ready."

They returned to their room and gathered their belongings. At least with minimal possessions, it did not take them long to be loaded up and on their way. The additional journey time and a stay in a strange bed had not dulled the Crawfords' mood. In fact, it seemed to have buoyed them.

Hannah glanced at Red to see his jaw twitching. Every now and then she gave his arm a squeeze, much like she had before, willing him to remain polite and quiet. She did most of the talking but Red's silence did not go unnoticed.

"You are terribly quiet today, my lord," Lady Crawford observed. "Was your room not to your liking? Bad night perhaps?"

"I slept like the dead," Lord Crawford declared.

"That you did," his wife agreed. "You were out within an instant, your mouth wide open like a frog wanting to catch flies."

Hannah giggled at the image.

"I slept well enough," Red said.

"Travelling does weary one, though," Hannah put in. Why Red could not make an excuse for himself, she did not know. She wished he would, even if it was a lie.

"Not to worry, we have a little stop planned at this charming village in which I grew up," Lady Crawford said with a smile. "It was where I met my dear Lord Crawford. He lured me away from it but whenever we go through, I insist on stopping to admire it." She sighed. "It has the most charming village green, and the church is medieval. You will think it quite charming, Miss St. John, I am certain of that."

"And by that, my wife means you must love it or else she shall be in a sulk for the rest of the day."

The viscountess shook her head. "He is a tease. I would never sulk. But I confess part of me always wishes visitors to adore it as much as I. Which is, of course, impossible because they never grew up there."

Hannah focused her attention on the passing countryside. Slowly, as they had moved inland, it had grown greener with more trees and hazel bushes sprouting up on the roadsides and dissecting the fields. The roads wound up hills, then back down them, and they passed some farmer's cottages, tucked carefully between the fields. Sheep were scattered across some but most looked to be for crop.

She knew when they were nearing the village as Lady Crawford could scarce keep still. They entered what was indeed a charming village, with white cottages lining the main street through it. The green sat ahead and the carriage drew to a stop by it. One wide oak tree occupied the center of the grass and cast its leafy shade wide across it.

Lady Crawford pushed herself out of her seat. "I must visit the village shop. They do the best fudge in all of England. Will you join us or perhaps you would prefer to stretch your legs? The earl needs a little something to lift his spirits I think."

"A little walk would do us good, thank you."

"Excellent." The viscount beamed. "We shan't be long." He laughed. "Well, we might be if my wife wishes to converse with every member of the village, but I vow to hasten her along."

Hannah and Red opted to stroll across the green toward the old oak tree. She ran her hands across the old bark, still sturdy and strong, even with a few names carved into it, some with love hearts etched clumsily around them, others written just to let people know they were there. She traced the shape of one lopsided heart. How long had it been there? Were the couple still in love or had time changed that?

"What shall you do after London?"

She turned to peer at Red. The question should not have surprised her but they had talked so little about their lives after this event. "Return home, of course."

"And?"

"Does there have to be an *and*?"

A smile quirked his lips. "Nothing is ever so simple with you, Hannah. Will you do more work for your father? Am I to expect you to crop up in Cornwall once more, demanding my aid?"

She shook her head. "Father has recovered a few artifacts, but none are as important as the stone. They can wait for transport."

Clouds drifted lazily across the sun, turning what had been a relatively clear day grey. She tucked herself under the shadows of the oak branches and tilted her head to eye Red.

"What of you? You will resume smuggling I suppose."

"That is the plan."

"Back to a life of crime."

"If that is how you want to think of it."

"It is not up to me how I think of it. The law says it's a crime."

"The law is often wrong."

She laughed. "It is wrong on many occasions. However, I do not think there is any moral argument for smuggling. It is used to line the pockets of unscrupulous men."

And sometimes she forgot this about Red. He might be an earl. He might look every inch the gentleman in his necktie and beautifully cut waistcoat and jacket. He was a smuggler, and she should remember that.

He took a step closer, entering the shelter of the trees and invading her space. He did it deliberately, she decided. The slow step forward, the way his eyes somehow darkened, the intense expression, and how he towered over her. Well, perhaps he could not help his height but the rest was intentional.

Whether he was trying to intimidate or something else, was another thing. The flutter in her stomach was not from fear that was for certain so if he was trying to make her see him as dark and dangerous, he was failing. No, when he came close all she could think on was his lips to her skin or on her mouth. Warmth rushed through her like that rogue wave that had nearly drowned him. But it did not leave her scared and gasping for breath.

She did tremble, though.

"You think me unscrupulous?"

"Of course," she said matter-of-factly. "Look at what I know of you, Red. You deliberately and quite obviously flout the law, and you are entirely proud of it."

"Am I?"

Her back connected with the bark, and she lifted her chin to meet his gaze. He rested a palm upon the tree trunk, almost imprisoning her. He need only place his free hand on the other side, and she would be his prisoner. Hannah drew in a breath.

A willing prisoner at that, she decided. There was no

denying it. Rogue or not, she wanted more kisses from him and certainly wanted to be in his embrace. Red was so complex, so mystifying, it was surely the only way to learn more.

"I think you take pride in your lawlessness, yes."

"So Miss Hannah St. John has me marked as the worst of men." His gaze was no longer on hers but following the line of her mouth and occasionally dropping to her neck and the rise of her breasts. She could feel her breathing quicken in response.

"Not the worst of men, no. You do not murder or take advantage of the weak." She smiled. "At least I hope you do not."

"I certainly do not." That other hand finally came up to capture her, holding her in place against the tree.

She could duck out if she really wished, but she did not. Never before had a person fascinated her so. The only time she ever felt so excited and captivated by something was when she was studying the stone. Even then, that had not made her legs feel like custard and her head swim with anticipation. There was, realistically, no comparison to being in Red's company.

"If I were really so unscrupulous," he murmured. "I would have taken you to bed on that first night."

"There was no bed," she pointed out, before she had even processed his words.

When they struck, they struck her hard. All words and rational thought fled her. Had he really been thinking of bedding her? Wishing he was wrapped in her embrace? It was the first time he had given voice to the attraction between them and even then she had not realized he had felt it so keenly.

"I am very inventive," he drawled.

"Helpful trait when one is a smuggler I suppose." The

lightness in her voice did not match the weight in her chest. It would only be relieved by a kiss or a touch. An embrace perhaps.

Him taking her to bed?

She shook her head. No, she had not come on this journey for that. This was about history, not some base need. It did not matter that she wanted to learn more of him and perhaps, even herself. She had always considered herself above desire for another person. No one had ever sparked such a thing inside her.

Until Red.

He leaned closer. "If I were a different man, I would have spent all of this journey showing you all of my helpful traits."

"You are assuming that I wanted to see them."

He chuckled. "You do. You would have done. Hannah, even you and all your logic could not deny it."

"I don't need to deny anything."

Red took a sudden step back. "So tell me, in all your logic, what do the facts present you? What do you feel toward me? What is this? Will you tell me you observe nothing between us?"

CHAPTER NINETEEN

R ed held his breath as he waited for a response. This entire experience since he had stepped off the carriage and walked toward the tree had been wholly unplanned. He'd gone with his gut, and it had led him down this bloody merry path. What would he do if she denied what was between them?

What would he do if she acknowledged it?

Nothing had changed. She was to go return to Hampshire and bury herself in her studies, and he had smuggling to do. The war effort relied on him, and he would not abandon that.

"My logic says..." She drew in a breath. "My logic says this is fleeting desire. That you want me because I am the nearest available woman, and you have been on the road for a while."

He smirked. "What of you? Is that your excuse?"

"I am not..." she lowered her voice, "I am not some sort of loose woman."

"Hannah, I do not think anyone would ever think that of you." He lifted his gaze to the gathering grey clouds that were rolling up aggressively. They would need to return to the coach shortly, but he would not leave this damned tree until this was resolved. "So you have never desired a man before?"

"No."

Why her response surprised him and filled him with pride, he did not know. Hannah would not desire lightly or easily, of course she would not, but to think he was the first man she had felt this way about...Damn, it was quite a responsibility.

He turned his full attention on her, stepping close once more. "You have me marked as quite a savage of a man, do you not?"

A crease appeared between her brows. "How so?"

"That you would think I only desire you because you are the nearest available woman."

"Well, I—"

"I can assure you, I am quite in control of myself. I do not desire every woman I see, and I do not need to satisfy myself at every moment. I am not a savage nor do I let my needs control me."

"Oh."

"Yes, oh." He let the realization sink in for a few moments. Why he had even started this conversation, he had little idea, only that since this morning when he had tasted her skin, he had been driven wild by the unspoken need between them. It had to be addressed, if only for his sanity.

After all, they both knew nothing could come of it.

He had not noticed the rain until a drop broke through the trees and landed on Hannah's cheek. Red lifted a finger to swipe it away but it was joined by several more. The rain pelted the tree, the noise amplified by the leaves. He grabbed Hannah's hand.

"We had better make a run for it."

She nodded, and they darted across the green. The sudden downpour had left the grass slick underfoot, and she nearly skidded and fell, so he snatched her up in his arms and carried her to the carriage. Once he had her deposited in the safety of the vehicle, he climbed in and shook the raindrops from his hat. Hannah undid her bonnet and did the same, straightening out the ribbon. She refused to look at him.

"Hannah—"

"Oh what fun!" Lady Crawford clambered into the coach, sending it rocking on its wheels. "Goodness, what is this English weather about? I do declare it will always take me by surprise, and you would think we English are used to the rain."

Her husband clambered in beside her. "Had to make a dash for it, did we not? My wife would have loved me to be as heroic as you, Redmere, but alas, I am not so strong as I was in my youth."

"And I am not so light." The viscountess laughed. "Our earl is quite the man, is he not?" she asked Hannah. "Scooping you up and getting you to safety. You are lucky to have a cousin like him."

Hannah smiled absently. "I am indeed."

The rain continued to patter on the roof of the coach, making conversation difficult as they continued their journey. The sound combined with the general rattling noise of their vehicle drowned out most of what the viscount and viscountess said so after several failed attempts on their behalf to strike conversation, they gave up and spoke amongst themselves.

Hannah remained quiet and thoughtful. It had not been his intention to make her feel uncomfortable, but he took some sick pleasure in the fact that she was now as preoccupied as he had been for most of their journey with the attraction between them.

The peacefulness of their journey was broken when they entered the outskirts of Taunton. The sprawling town consisted mostly of Tudor cottages with newer houses surrounding them. The mix of clean, square and modern buildings next to old, crooked black and white houses was an intriguing combination but it seemed to work. The church tower dominated the skyline, its red brick striking a stark contrast to all the white and cream painted walls.

They rolled over a bridge that crossed the River Tone—a wide stretch of water that flowed rapidly with the sudden downpour and extra rain they had likely been experiencing with the rest of the south of England.

Red had travelled through Taunton a few times. It was the easiest stop on a journey to London from Cornwall, but he usually only stopped briefly. Hannah did not know it yet, but he intended for them to stay more than a night. He could not bear to see her in the same gown over and over. Not that he cared much for what women wore, but he could tell it aggravated her to be seen as messy and dirty. Once they found a room at an inn, he would set about seeing if he could not arrange a new wardrobe.

The carriage came to a halt in the market square. The remnants of market stalls remained with scraps of paper and food littering the cobbled square.

"There's a fine inn just there." Lord Crawford motioned across to a large inn, each window lit, ready for the encroaching evening. "Very good food and excellent beds. We stayed there when Fanny was suffering a malady."

"You will be quite comfortable there, though my cousin would not mind at all if you came to stay with us," the viscountess insisted.

Red shook his head. "We could not impose, particularly with no notice."

"She would not mind a jot, but I understand your reticence." Lady Crawford grinned. "Such a gentleman."

Beside him, Hannah snorted and then tried to conceal it

with a cough. He lifted a brow and looked at her, but she avoided his gaze.

"Well, do stop by if you are ever in the area again," Lord Crawford said as Red picked up the stone.

"Absolutely." The viscount had ensured Red knew well where he lived should he ever wish to visit. Red could hardly see that ever happening. "Thank you for your help. You have, no doubt, made our journey much easier."

Lady Crawford beamed at Hannah. "You will not have a problem hiring a private coach from here. You shall soon be in London and no doubt enjoying yourselves wonderfully. Goodness, it almost makes me wish I was a young girl again."

"Take care of yourselves, Lord and Lady Crawford," Hannah said. "We are very grateful for your help."

The viscount waved a hand once they'd climbed out of the carriage. "Happy to help. Enjoy London!"

A heavy weight lifted off Red's shoulders once the carriage disappeared between a chandlery and a shoemaker's. He huffed out a breath.

"They were not that bad."

"I do not do well in company."

Hannah looked at him quizzically. "You do well in my company."

"Yours is an exception, and the Crawfords were quite the handful."

"I imagine you prefer the company of your, um, smuggling friends."

"They are hard-working, decent men, and they know when to leave me in peace. Three excellent qualities." He hefted his bag over his shoulder and cradled the stone against his chest.

"Decent? I do not think I have ever heard a smuggler being called decent."

"In spite of your assumptions, they are good men,

Hannah." He nodded toward the inn. "Shall we get a room or are we to stand here discussing your judgements of my companions all day?"

"They are not judgements," she protested, scurrying along behind him as he strode toward the front door set directly in the center of the building. "How can being a smuggler and being decent go hand in hand? It's not logical. A decent man would not smuggle."

"And I am not decent?"

"Well, I...no, I mean yes. I mean..." She sighed.

Red pushed open the door for her and escorted her in. Neither of them were unused to traveler's inns and the general business of them as well as some of the more unsavory characters they attracted on the road. However, this inn took Red by surprise. From the outside it was a large building and well looked after with recently painted shutters, beams and walls, but aside from that it looked like any other inn.

Inside, though, they were greeted with beautiful woodwork on the walls, freshly polished and gleaming. The bar did not hold the usual scratches and stains, housing only a row of polished tankards at one end and a jar of pickled eggs on the other end. There was no stench of stale sweat and ale, and the room instead gave off a fragrance of earthy hops and herbs.

It was indeed busy, but the patrons were not like the mixed lot that they had encountered so far. Most were as well dressed as he, if a little less road-weary. The women wore silks and had fine embroidery on their gowns and feathers in their hair. He glanced at Hannah to see she had noted the state of the guests here. She looked down at her own gown and bit her lip.

Several guests occupied the stalls in front of the bar,

forcing Red to push between them. A scrawny bar maid with a clean, fresh complexion smiled politely at him.

"Can I help, sir?"

"Yes, a room if you please."

"Aye, I'll be a moment." The girl vanished behind the bar and emerged out of a door at the other end of the room. She swept past the tables that were mostly full. Though she was dressed simply, she was clean and well-presented. Clearly there was money behind this inn.

"If you follow me," she motioned to the door to the right and pushed it open. They entered a reception room with a small desk. The carpets were thick under his feet and felt new.

She flicked open a book on the desk and pulled out a quill. "How many rooms would you like, sir?"

He paused. They had been sharing a room up until now, for Hannah's safety and his ease of mind really. It was hardly respectable but no one would know, so it hardly mattered. However, he doubted there was a single ruffian here, not when he spied their nightly rates pinned on the wall. No ruffian could afford such a place.

"Two rooms, if you please."

"Of course." The woman unhooked two keys from the hooks on the wall and handed them over. "You are on the top floor. If you follow the stairs up, your rooms are on the left." She motioned to the book. "If you could sign in, please."

Red nodded and signed them in as brother and sister under entirely false names. They had adopted such a false-hood for most of the journey, but he had not been bothered about using his own name until now. There was a chance there would be people who would at least recognize his name if they saw it in the book and they would know full well he had no sister or sister-in-law.

Red led the way and opened Hannah's room first, ushering her in. He eyed the room. It was simplistic but clean and more spacious than what they had stayed in previously. A brass bed was pushed up against one wall with its blankets tucked in neatly. The vanity table was of dark wood and highly polished. There was an armoire for her clothes too—not that she had any.

"Pleasant room," he murmured.

"You trust me on my own finally?"

"I thought you could do without my snoring disturbing you, and this seems a decent establishment." He let slip a smile. "I do not think you can get into any trouble here."

She returned his smile. "Is that a challenge?"

"Absolutely not. We have had a run of rotten luck, but it seems to be changing. Let us not test that." He carried the stone over to the vanity table. Before he could put it down, the fabric around it loosened and his grip failed. He squeezed the artifact tighter, but it slipped. Even in his frantic struggle to grab it, he failed. Searing pain burst through his foot and the stone balanced briefly on his toes then crashed down to one side.

Snatching his foot from underneath the rock, he hopped about. "Shit, shit, shit, shit." He couldn't even begin to care about his language in front of Hannah.

She scurried to his side and urged him onto the bed. "Does it hurt?"

"Of course it bloody well hurts."

"Sit down." Her features were etched with concern.

"I am bloody sitting."

She knelt in front of him and worked off his boot. He sucked in a breath through his teeth as his toe throbbed impatiently. Hannah gingerly pulled away his sock and her tiny distressed noise made his foot ache all the more. He finally looked down at the damage and grimaced. His big toe was twice the size it should have been and the toe next to it had caught some of the blow too.

"It might be broken," Hannah said. "Can you wriggle it?"

He was able to though it made him wince.

"You may still have a fracture. In fact, I would think it likely with the weight of the artifact."

"Bloody thing," he grumbled.

"It will not stop you walking on it though it might be sore for some time." She glanced up at him. "Is it very painful?"

He pressed his lips together and pushed up from the bed. "I've suffered worse."

Certainly he had suffered plenty of bumps and scrapes over the years, particularly once he'd embarked into the smuggling trade, but he had never broken anything. The incessant throb was the worst of it and the knowledge that when it bruised, it would likely stiffen and make walking that much harder. Just what he needed.

Hannah lifted both hands and tried to persuade him to sit back down.

He fixed her with a look. "You need a wash and a rest no doubt. And I will dunk this in some cold water, see if that helps."

"Should I see if the kitchen has any ice or cold steaks?"

He shook his head. "I don't need a bloody fuss. Just a few moments."

She peered at the stone and then back at him. "I am sorry."

"It was my damned fault, but I'll admit I'm surprised you are not scolding me for dropping the stone."

"You do think me heartless, do you not?"

"Obsessed more like."

A strange smile crossed her lips, one that was almost wistful. "Not at all."

Red thrust a finger at the abandoned artifact. "The sooner we get that blasted stone to London, the better."

Her smile vanished. If he were not hurting so badly, he might have tried to find out what he had done to upset her, but all he could do was snatch up his boot and sock and hobble to his room. She followed him out as though he might do something else foolish like tumble down the stairs or fall out of his bedroom window.

"You don't need to follow me," he snapped.

"I wanted to make sure you got to your room safely."

"I am next door to you, Hannah," he said through gritted teeth. "I can hardly get into much trouble." He fumbled with the key while balancing his bag on one arm and his boot and sock in the other hand. It clattered to the floor and he cursed.

Hannah dipped to get the key, opened his door without a word, and pressed it into his hand once he had stepped inside.

"Good night, Red."

"Are we not going to have dinner?"

"I think I shall eat in my room." She pulled the door shut before he could respond.

Red set about pouring water into the washbowl. He dipped a finger in it and found it to be nice and cold. Not ideal for bathing to be sure but perfect for his sore foot. He rolled up his breeches and set the bowl on the floor. Sucking in a breath, he submerged his swollen toe in the water. Wincing, he expelled the breath and forced himself to relax.

He would not, however, ponder as to why he had upset Hannah. He seemed to be good at that at the moment. Not long ago, that might have pleased him. Aggravating Miss St. John had been quite amusing. But that did not matter because he wasn't going to dwell on it. What did it matter if he had offended her a little? Even though he could not understand what it was he had done. After all, he hadn't dropped the stone on *her* toe. And he had not broken or damaged the artifact—at least he did not think so. If he had, she would have been fussing over the stupid stone instead of him, surely? So how had he upset her?

Red forced his attention to his pounding toe.

But why had her smile vanished at the mention of getting rid of the stone? Was it the idea of having to hand it over? If that was what it was about, she had no reason to be annoyed at him. He pinched the bridge of his nose. Miss Hannah St. John was causing him far too much aggravation. Somehow, deep down, he had this horrible suspicion the woman was worth it.

CHAPTER TWENTY

Hannah tried to awaken in a better mood, really she did. The bed had been the most comfortable she had slept on all week, and the room had been quiet with little noise coming up from the bar thanks to being on the top floor. There was no reason at all to be grumpy.

And she certainly had no reason to direct that grumpiness at Red. The man had been utterly clueless as to why she had been annoyed at him yesterday, and for that she was grateful because her reasoning was foolish and illogical.

What did it matter if he was desperate for their time together to be over? He had made no promises and neither had she. Why, what a fool she must be to think an earl-turned-smuggler would want anything from her.

Hannah splashed her face and dabbed away the droplets as they ran down her neck. She dressed in an efficient manner. If she kept herself busy enough, she would not think on Red and this strange emotional turmoil she had managed to tangle herself up in.

"Silly girl," she muttered to her reflection while she ran a brush through her hair. "Silly, silly girl."

She had been hurt. There, she admitted it. Red had hurt her. She scowled at herself. Somehow she had let Red in, and now he had the ability to hurt her. In truth, she had not even realized she had been keeping people out until now, but apparently she had been. There was no sense in lying to herself.

But now she had let someone infiltrate and why? Because he was handsome? Intelligent? Because he could trade words with her so beautifully and encouraged her to be something more than just an intellect?

She stuck out her tongue at her reflection. No more dwelling on this. It would not help. Red wanted to return home and rightly so. He had a smuggling operation to see to and she...well she would go home and wait for her father, she supposed. Hopefully he would return from France before long and they could discuss all that he had recovered.

They would be apart, and that was how it should be. Red was simply a sensible man, while she was being utterly insensible. A strange thing for her to be sure, but she would conquer it. She would remind herself at every moment that there was nothing apart from a mild attraction between her and Red and he would return to Cornwall soon and forget her.

And she would forget him.

She narrowed her gaze at herself. "Yes, you will."

Hannah dressed and started her hair. She would try to make it as pretty as possible to make up for the fact she was wearing a dress that had yet to be cleaned or pressed. Hopefully the liberal amount of scent of violets would freshen it up. It was hardly ideal, but how could she complain? It had been her fault.

She was just in the process of pushing in the last few clips when there was a knock at the door. A few clips pressed between her lips and one hand in her hair, she opened the door. Her heart gave a stutter.

Unlike her, Red was beautifully clean and well-presented. Elegant from his single-breasted grey waistcoat and slightly darker tailcoat to his buckskins. And there was she, looking as though she had just emerged from the workhouse.

"Good morning," he said, hesitation in his voice.

"Good morning," she murmured with the clips still between her lips. She glanced at his shoe as though she could see through it and know the condition of his foot. "How is your toe?"

"Better. Though I have perfected an excellent hobble."

"So it is still sore?"

He lifted a shoulder. "I'll survive."

"I am sorry."

"It was my fault." He searched her face. "It was my fault, Hannah," he insisted.

Likely he thought she'd been upset by what had happened to his toe. Certainly she regretted he had been hurt by the artifact, but that was not what had disturbed her.

"Anyway," he grinned at her, "I thought I might take you into town and we could eat there."

"Of course. Let me finish my hair." She turned, and he ducked into her room. The space instantly grew smaller. As she sat and pushed the clips into place, picking up a butterfly comb to finish it.

Hannah fumbled it, and the comb fell on the floor. Before she could bend to pick it up, Red had appeared at her side. He straightened, comb in hand. "Allow me."

She motioned to the back of her hair where the curls were gathered. "Just here."

Never taking his gaze from hers, he slid the comb into place and adjusted it several times to his liking. He admired his own work in the mirror. "Perfect."

Had she had any breath left in her body, it would have frozen. As it was, it had vanished as soon as his fingers had come to her hair. A bitter ache gathered in her throat. She tore her gaze away and stood abruptly, forcing Red to take several steps back. Snatching up her pelisse, she slung it on, avoiding his aid and lifted her chin to meet his gaze.

"Shall we?"

"Of course." There was confusion in his eyes, likely over her abrupt manner.

But how was he to know she had spent the night thinking of him, wondering why it was she did not wish to leave his side so soon. Pondering how it would be possible for a blue-stocking and a smuggler to be together. Dwelling on utterly fanciful notions.

She did not like it once bit. She dealt with facts, not fancy. And the facts were, he had expressed nothing but mild attraction toward her. He was a smuggler. He lived a less than savory life. He was arrogant and a tease. Not to mention he was an earl. She might be a gentleman's daughter, but she hardly ranked high enough to pass an earl's notice.

Red took her arm once they were downstairs and out in the street. It had rained overnight, leaving puddles between the cobbles. A carriage rattled past, overloaded with passengers and parceled goods. She had to dart back so as not to get sprayed with water as its wheel hit a water-loaded rut. She was already dirty and creased, but she did not want it to get much worse. Hopefully she might find a washerwoman or someone at the inn to scrub her dress overnight so at least she could be clean again before they moved on.

"Did you sleep well?" Red asked as he led her along the crowded pavement.

The hour was early but not so early as to dissuade people from strolling along the main street. Shops lined it, some of them with their goods spilling onto the street. The haberdashery had so many fabrics that it had a stall set up in front displaying the vibrant colors and beautiful fabrics. A few street vendors offered their wares on the edge of the road. The scent of roasted chestnuts reached her nose, and she spied the smoke from the stall up ahead.

"Excellently," she lied.

"Good."

"And you?"

"Not so well."

Her heart gave a little jolt. Had he been thinking of her too? "Oh. Why?"

He glanced down at his hobbling gait. "Having a toe twice the size as it should be is a little off-putting." He motioned along the street to a narrow building that looked as if it had been squeezed between the other two at one point. It had two windows at the bottom and a small pale blue door. All the woodwork has been painted to match. It reached up to three stories and hanging beneath the second set of windows was a sign indicating it was a tea room.

"This is an excellent place to eat."

She nodded, too hungry and on edge to question his decision. It did indeed look pleasant, so she was happy to let him take charge. He opened the door and urged her in with a palm to her back. It occurred to her that this was not a lone moment. There had been many a time when he had taken her arm or touched her in some familiar way. She had become so used to it, these moments had barely passed her notice, but for some reason, it did now.

It really did.

Her back felt scalded by the touch, and she instantly missed it when his palm left her.

She ducked into the room. The low beams were hardly low enough to hit her head, but they left the room feeling tiny. Underfoot, the floorboards were uneven and left one feeling as though one were on board a ship as they made their way to a table in the corner. Several tables were already full with a crowd of well-to-do patrons enjoying tea, scones and cream.

"And here I thought only Devon was known for its scones and cream," she remarked as she sat.

"Apparently Somerset likes the tradition too."

A young man, no older than six and ten bustled over. An apron tied around his waist, he had smears of what appeared to be jam on it and a ruddy complexion that nearly blended in with his bright red hair.

"What can I get you, sir, ma'am?"

Hannah peered at the board on the wall where what was on offer was meticulously listed. Then she eyed the scones at the table next to them. "Scones and cream, if you please. And some coffee."

Red grinned. "The same for me please. And plenty of coffee."

The young lad dipped his head and hastened off at a speed far too quick for so early in the morning. The simmering chatter around them indicated that most people had not quite awoken either and had come for the coffee in the hopes of it aiding them through the day.

"I thought..." Red leaned in, and Hannah frowned. There was a nervous air about him. So very unlike Red. "I thought we might visit a dressmaker or two today."

"We can hardly afford to wait weeks for new dresses to be made."

Was it silly of her to think that actually she would be willing to wait? Did it make her a fool to give up her plans simply so she could spend more time with Red before returning home? She drew in a breath and ran her finger across a scar in the wooden table. "Yes."

"Pardon?"

Hannah smiled hastily. "Nothing at all."

"So you do not wish to argue with me?" His lips quirked. "You might like to tell me that in some certain historical era it was considered a status symbol to remain in one's clothes forever? Or maybe you are hoping that the mud stains on your skirts will give you a superior air, as though you have just dug the stone from the ground yourself?"

Blast, she was flushing. He was right, she was muddy, and the chances were, after another day, she could add smelly to that too. She could not stay in this dress forever, and if she didn't find someone who could wash it tonight, she would look even more like she had just emerged from the digs around the pyramids.

"I am sorry that I am a sight for sore eyes," she said primly. "I had intended to have it washed tonight if I could find someone."

Creases appeared around his eyes. "Hannah, I have seen you in a worst state. Our first night together you could be likened to a drowned rat, if you recall."

She shuddered. "Do not mention rats."

"My point is, I do not care if you wish to walk around like some creature from the deep, but I am sure you do."

The young lad interrupted, nearly dropping the first plate of scones in his haste. Red grabbed the plate quickly and prevented it from spilling all over Hannah's lap. The boy mumbled several apologies and placed a jug of coffee and cups on their table.

"I do not suppose a bit of cream and jam could have made much difference to my appearance at this point."

"You would look tastier to be certain."

Hannah giggled. "You cannot tell me you do not mind that you are travelling with a creature who looks as though she may have been pulled from a gutter. It is not very becoming of an earl."

"I long ago gave up caring what others thought."

Slathering her scone in cream and jam, she took a bite whilst Red poured the coffee. The sweet bite of the strawberry, mingling with the delicate, indulgent taste of the cream made her close her eyes. Combined with the strong scent of coffee, she could almost forget she was in a crusty, old gown, feeling entirely unattractive in front of the most attractive man she had ever met.

"Nice?"

She snapped open her eyes to find Red staring at her with that intense look that was becoming more frequent. She swiped away some cream from the corner of her lip and licked it off the end of her finger before nodding. His expression became slightly pained.

"If you wish to see if we can find me a dress," she conceded, unwilling to annoy him further, "we can try. However, I do not see what we can do in a short space of time. We should be arranging a carriage today."

His attention snapped away from her mouth, and he took a gulp of coffee. Red cursed, nearly dropping the coffee and letting it slop over the side of the cup as he slammed it down.

"Hot?"

He nodded. "We'll find you a dress," he assured. "I'll be damned if I have reputation for being able to get hold of anything for nothing."

"If we are to wait for you to smuggle one in from France," she said, her voice low, "then we shall have a long stay here indeed."

He leaned in, his smile wicked. "You underestimate my bargaining skills, Miss St. John. Whatever you need I can get."

Hannah was not at all sure what she needed at present, or whether he could get it for her.

CHAPTER TWENTY-ONE

Red could not help feel a little smug when the dressmaker had promised Hannah two new dresses in two days. Of course, his pocketbook had helped persuade the woman to readjust some nearly completed gowns to fit Hannah and delay giving them to the original intended owner. The woman took Hannah aside to get her measurements, so Red stepped out of the small shop. Being surrounded by lace and fabrics was not his idea of fun, and he'd far rather be out in the fresh air.

The town bustled as lunchtime dawned. Most carriages travelling through the south stopped here, assured of excellent service and food, as well as a chance of running into fine company. He cared little for the company, but he hoped Hannah appreciated the food and good services. They would have had little chance of finding her some new clothes in the smaller towns.

She had seemed on better form since he had suggested getting her a new gown or two and he was certain she had enjoyed the scones and cream. Lord knows he had, but mostly because she had been sitting opposite him with the wildest expression of bliss on her face. Hell, he'd burned his mouth because he had been staring at her for too long, and when she had put her finger in her mouth to lick off the cream...Jesus, he was as hard as stone.

"Well, I'll be damned."

It was probably not a bad thing he had been interrupted from his reverie or else he would be making a fool of himself right here in the main street. He certainly did not expect to see Harry Coolidge. It had to have been over a year since he had seen him.

"Harry," Red said, extending a hand.

The man shook his warmly. The year had not been kind to Harry, but that was likely because of his wartime experiences. He had aged since he had ferried him across from France at the dead of night. It had been one of the few journeys that Red had decided he could be of more help on deck rather than at home, waiting by the coast. The English spy had been injured and was in possession of important information on Napoleon's next moves. What they were, Red couldn't say—only Harry ever knew the information he possessed—but with him suffering a nasty wound to the leg, they had brought him directly into London, slipping past the customs men by running dark. There were French spies everywhere, as they were all too well aware. Harry was probably the most precious cargo they had ever shipped.

"How goes it?" Red asked. He peered up into eyes that were creased and ringed with dark circles. A hint of grey touched Harry's sideburns. "Still in the business?"

Harry shook his head and tapped his leg with a cane. "Hardly up to it anymore. It caused some mighty damage and still pains me when the weather is bad. Still the crown gave me a nice retirement fund so I cannot complain, though I shall confess being idle is a strange business."

"You could always join me in Cornwall. I could keep you busy."

"But for how long, Red? The war will come to an end eventually. Don't tell me you shall remain a smuggler for the rest of your days."

He shrugged. "Perhaps I shall."

Harry smirked. "You act the rogue, but we all know why you do what you do. Were it not for the war, you would never have even considered such an occupation."

Red did not deny it. Were it not for Nate and his ambitions to help the war cause, perhaps he might not have thought to do a thing. He was not heartless—the men losing their lives for a cause they likely did not understand bothered him aplenty—but as a titled man, there was little he could do except donate charitably to the soldiers and their widows.

"What are you doing in Taunton anyway? A little far from Cornwall for you. I know how you loathe to be anywhere but the very end of the country."

Hannah emerged from the dressmaker's and came to his side. He naturally extended his arm, and she took it. To have her next to him or near him was becoming as normal as breathing. It would be odd indeed to have her gone.

"May I introduce Miss St. John. I am escorting her to London."

"Ah," was all Harry said.

Red narrowed his eyes, fully understanding his friend's assumption. He thought Red had been lured away from Cornwall by the flick of a petticoat.

"This is Mr. Harry Coolidge. An old friend," Red explained.

Hannah swung her gaze between the two men and smiled. "A pleasure to meet you, Mr. Coolidge. How is it you know Red?"

"Socially," Red interrupted. "We spent time together a few years ago."

A crease appeared between her brows. "I see."

"Well, I had better leave you two to your shopping," Harry said, bowing his head. "It was a pleasure to meet you, Miss St. John. Do look after Red here for me."

"Of course."

"Take care, Harry." Red shook his hand and watched him walk away, his limp only just noticeable. It made Red feel ridiculous for hobbling along with a swollen toe.

"So you met a few years ago?" Hannah quizzed.

"Something like that."

"Where exactly?"

Red led Hannah along the street, intending to take them back to the inn for luncheon. "I cannot recall."

"And yet Mr. Coolidge seemed so fond of you. Were the feelings not reciprocated?"

"I consider Harry an excellent friend."

"But you do not recall where you met? Or what you did to become good friends?"

He scowled. "No."

"Why do you insist on playing the rogue, Red, when it is becoming quite clear you are the opposite?"

"I am not sure where you got the idea that I am some sort of fine gentleman, but I can assure you, you are wrong."

She tugged him to a halt. "No, *you* are wrong. I do not think of you as some sort of fine gentleman. You have your moments but you are mostly coarse and rude and you take some absurd pleasure in it. But I also do know you do not have the sort of hard heart you seem to wish you had."

"Hannah, you are talking in riddles. Now, I am hungry and I should like to get a seat at the inn, but if we dally any longer, we shall be lucky to find a haystack to sit upon."

"I heard what Harry said," she replied softly, looking up at him from under her lashes.

"Pardon?"

"I heard what he said. About you helping the war effort. I will admit, I have spent most of journey pondering over why a man like you would take up smuggling." She grinned. "It all makes sense now. You use it to cover taking over spies."

Red hauled in a breath. He spied a nearby bench, tucked against a backdrop of leafy trees and a stretch of grass that was no doubt covered in picnic blankets during better weather. He sat and motioned for her to sit next to him.

"We take over goods too and bring them back. Sometimes we supply the soldiers when our warships cannot get supplies across. No one questions the presence of smugglers. And of course, we take information."

She opened her mouth, closed it, then opened it again. "Why did you not just tell me?"

"What I do is dangerous, Hannah, not simply because of the excise men. Spies like Harry rely on my secrecy to continue their activities. Were it not for his injury, the chances were, I would have been shipping him back over to continue his mission. Anyway, what difference would it have made if I told you?"

She tilted her head. "I am not sure."

"I still smuggle. I bring in goods that we would not otherwise have access to in England. I make a profit."

"So now you are trying to convince me that you are still a rogue?"

"No, I am merely pointing out that I am only human, not a saint. My method works, but it works twofold. In a time of uncertainty, these profits are ensuring my estate thrives, and I cannot complain about the consequence of my actions."

"Why did you decide to do this?"

"My brother intended to join the army, and it was my

father's ambition for him too. Unfortunately, after my father passed, my brother's eyesight deteriorated. It is not so bad, but he has to have glasses so he cannot purchase a commission. At least this way, he can feel he is doing something to help. Being a first son can mean a great deal of pressure, but being a second son can leave one adrift. I have seen it many times. I did not wish that for Nate."

A soft smile curved her lips. "And now you have persuaded me you are no longer a rogue but simply a caring brother. Which one do you wish to be, Red? Rogue or gentleman?"

He didn't say it but right at that moment, he wished to be the rogue. To tell her of his deepest desires and how her small smile made him want to tip her off this bench and kiss her until she begged him for more. Unfortunately for him, but most likely fortunately for her, the gentleman was here for the day.

CHAPTER TWENTY-TWO

Hannah had almost expected something to prevent them from hiring a private coach. Goodness, she had already hoped something would. After waiting two days for her promised dresses, they were on their way. The weather was fine and dry, the coach in excellent condition and Red's toe had reduced in size. Their drivers were capable and the horses in excellent health. She now wore a dress of cotton and silk in a lemon yellow. The skirts were full and the bodice high, pinched in with an elegant broach detail under the bust. It was quite the relief to be out of her lone dress.

Red offered a smile in her direction as the carriage moved at a fair pace. If all went smoothly, they would be in London in three days.

Three days.

She propped her chin on her hand and an elbow on the open window to watch the scenery pass by. The hills were gentler here in Somerset than in Devon or Cornwall. Like a rolling sea, they rose and lowered in careful arcs, dotted with lines of trees and hedges that segmented the farmer's fields.

So much of her wanted their journey to last longer which

was ridiculous. She hardly minded travelling, but it had never been her favorite thing in the world. It had always been the destination that had excited her. Finding somewhere new, learning about it, and uncovering history she had never known of before.

Of course, the man next to her had much of an influence on her sudden liking for travelling. He had accused her of likely seeing him differently had she known about his activities when they had first met, but she didn't think that was true. His arrogance would still have grated on her and his ability to pick so perfectly on the things that would aggravate her would have riled her.

Nothing had changed. He was still the same man. And yet, no matter how often she reminded herself that, she could not fail to deny that everything had changed. Perhaps *she* had changed. Her lone focus was no longer the stone. Her passions had diverted. As much as she wanted to unlock the secrets behind the stone, it was not the only thing she wanted. She supposed that for once in her life, she wanted something for herself.

And that something was Red.

She sighed. What a conundrum. If she had ever thought she would fall for someone, she never thought it would be a smuggling earl. No, he would have had a brilliant mind, a passion for history but also a passion for her. None of those brilliant men she had met so far had been capable of passion for other people. Perhaps she had not either until now.

"We shall be in Hampshire by tomorrow," Red said.

She nodded.

Naturally, Red had a brilliant mind. Only a truly clever man could run an operation as he did. He did not have a passion for history perhaps, but he had a passion for helping his brother and the war effort. That was certainly to be admired.

Yes, maybe her feelings for him had changed, but it was nothing to do with her new knowledge. She had been aware of the creeping sensation for at least two days. It slowly consumed her mind, changed it and twisted it. If she thought hard about it, studied herself closely, she was awfully afraid that if she was not already, she might be half in love with him.

"Shall we travel near your home?" he pressed, drawing her from her thoughts and the realization that was making her frown.

"I have some family near Winchester, but my Father's house is in Alresford which is a little farther down the county."

"I know of it though I have never had occasion to visit it."

"It is but a small town. Few people have a reason to pass through."

"I do not venture from Cornwall often. As we know, the journey is not an easy one." He grinned, and she chuckled.

"I shall confess I have had less trouble visiting the farthest reaches of Scotland. I think I would rather conquer the Highland mountains than attempt that journey again."

"So you shall never visit Cornwall again?"

The way he said it left a hollow ache in her chest. "Oh no, that's not what I—that is, if I have occasion to, I certainly would. Cornwall is a beautiful place."

Oh dear, now she had made him think she did not like his home or that she never wished to see him again. It was what she had feared he had meant when he wanted the journey over. Perhaps he still did. She could hardly be sure. The way he had spoiled her with dresses and cream teas, she had considered that she might have misunderstood. But then, he was essentially a gentleman no matter how much he tried to be the rogue. It could have simply been him being gentlemanly.

"I have a fondness for it, of course." His smile was wistful. "The best society tends to avoid it. Not exciting enough for them, I suspect."

"Not everyone needs excitement. I think we have had enough to last for a lifetime."

He nodded. "We certainly have. Though I could not think of another person I would have rather experienced it with."

"Even our dreadful ferry experience?"

"No," he said firmly. "I never, ever want to see you on a ferry in such waters again. I thought you were to go overboard." He grinned. "And, of course, if I had rescued you and ignored the stone, I would likely have found myself in even deeper waters."

She tapped his arm. "Even I know the stone is not worth my life. Though I might have been tempted to dive for it in better weather," she admitted. "My father might not have been very understanding. I do not suppose any of his finds have caused him quite so much trouble."

"Ah. So you do think it's cursed."

"Not at all. We simply had a run of bad luck. Curses do not exist."

"Because they are not logical."

"Precisely."

"But luck exists?"

She shook her head. "It is just a saying. A string of bad things happened to us, completely coincidentally."

His smiled softened. "You have an excellent way of explaining things, Hannah. Sometimes, however, things cannot be explained."

His gaze locked onto hers, and she felt as though he must be able to see right into her thoughts. Deep, deep into them, digging out her secrets, her feelings for him. Her body practically screamed at him to kiss her. How obvious she had to be.

The coach came to an abrupt stop, forcing her to grip the door. She went to pop her head out, but Red pulled her back to her seat.

"Stay where you are," he ordered. His body was tense, his jaw tight.

Hannah's heart gave a jolt. She knew what he feared. Highwaymen.

He eased open the door and climbed out. She twined her hands in her lap, aware of the murmurs of men and her heart pounding so hard that it made her palms clammy. She could not hear what was being said but there was no shouting or demands to hand over any goods, just the low conversation of Red and the driver. What was happening?

After several more tense moments, Hannah gave up waiting. If it was a highwayman, surely something would have happened by now? She popped her head and nearly fell back to her seat at the sight that greeted her. She peered out again and laughed.

A sea of cows covered the road, hemmed in by the bushes on either side. There had to be at least twenty of them. They were stood in a face-off with Red and the other men. Slowly the cows were encroaching on them, surrounding them. There was no aggression behind the animal's movement, but none of the men could persuade the beasts to move.

Hannah pushed open the door and stepped out. Red did not spot her until she was in front of the carriage. By then, he was hemmed in and unable to move in any direction.

"Hannah, what are you doing?" he called.

She pressed a finger to her lips. "Shhh."

She eyed the first cow in front of her. The animal blinked lazily at her and shuffled slightly forward. Hannah put out a hand. "You are a lovely lady, are you not?" she said softly. "What a lovely lady," she cooed.

There were no calves, and it was early in the day. The

cows were likely just curious and not feeling at all protective. As long as no one began shouting, they could be assured of remaining safe.

The cow nudged forward slightly and her nose connected with Hannah's hand. The animals were well-used to humans which was a blessing. She rose onto tiptoes and spotted the open gate in which they had likely emerged from. Unless they managed to move them, their journey could be delayed for quite some time.

She spoke to the animal, low and soft. The other men remained frozen, watching and waiting for her to make a move. Once she could be sure the cow was not concerned by her presence, she moved her hand along to the animal's shoulder blade and gave her nudge.

"Come then, girl. Time to move."

The animal shuffled slightly, moving to turn. The other animals were facing in various directions. Most had been quite content with filling the road and remaining there and had not been bothered by the carriage until the men had disembarked and given them something else to investigate. The movement of the one cow shifted the others around her. Hannah gave the animal another push and urged it to allow her to move between the animals and emerge slowly at the front. Once she started moving toward the gate, some of the other cows began to pay attention to her. She gave a few of them an encouraging push on the shoulder, and they all began to shift in the direction of the gate. The chances were they knew full well where they were meant to be, they just needed someone to give them some orders.

It was a painfully slow process. She motioned for the men to remain, but she could see Red was desperate to move to the head of the herd and help her. However, any sudden movements would have risked it all—including her life—and he likely knew that so remained where he was.

Once the last cow was in the field, she latched the gate and let herself relax. She had not felt particularly scared at the time, but once the tension left her, she realized she had been extremely fearful of a stampede.

Red rushed to her side and grabbed her waist. "Where the devil did you learn to herd cows?"

"My father and I live next to a dairy farm. I watched the farmer deal with the cattle many a time."

He hauled her close to him. "Thank the lord for your incessant need to study everything, though I'll tell you now, Hannah, you ever scare me like that again, I shall have to put you over my knee."

She felt herself flushing. "I didn't mean to scare you, but I could see you were getting nowhere with them."

Red motioned to the driver. "Let us move on before we encounter anymore animals."

He aided Hannah back into the coach. As soon as she had sat, he took her face in his hands. She stared at him, wide-eyed.

"Never scare me again."

"I will not," she promised, unsure why she was even vowing as much. How many more chances would she even have to scare him?

His stark expression softened. "I am so proud of you." He grinned. "Miss St. John, leader of cows."

She laughed. "I am not sure I want that title." A flush of warmth spread through her, though, at the thought of garnering his pride.

"Hannah, Queen of the Cows."

"No, I do not want that either."

"How about Hannah, the boldest, cleverest woman I ever did meet?"

"Now I like that."

"I could not stand to lose you, you know."

The intensity in his eyes made her stomach turn inside out. She drew in a breath and kept it there. Whatever did he mean? "I—"

"I feared I was going to lose you to cows." He smirked. "I'm not sure I could bear it."

"If I was trampled by cows?"

He shook his head. "No. Well, yes. But in general…"

Hannah tried to swallow down the knot in her throat. She longed to probe him more, but he looked as confused as she felt.

"Let's talk more in London."

Unable to summon a response, she nodded and settled back against her seat. Her gut was telling her something. If he could not stand to lose her…did that mean he wanted to keep her?

CHAPTER TWENTY-THREE

"Are you sure about this?"

Red's brow lifted. "Of course. Why would I not be?"

Hannah tucked her bottom lip under her top teeth. "My aunt Ellen is a little eccentric." She paused. "I suppose much of my family is."

Truth be told, Red was keen to visit Hannah's family. It would give him a little insight into her life. All she talked of was her father and their adventures into the annals of history, but she never went further than that. How did she feel growing up motherless? Did she not wish she had a constant parent at times? When she had mentioned they were close to her aunt's, he thought it a fine opportunity to find out more.

"I hope she will not object to you being escorted around by me."

Hannah laughed as she picked up her new bag containing her old dress and the other one he had purchased. She had tried to offer him some money for them, but naturally he had refused. It was likely she had little idea how big a bribe he had used to ensure they had those dresses with haste.

"What's so funny?" He hefted the stone into his hold.

"Aunt Ellen is not one for propriety. You shall see what I mean."

He had to wonder quite what he was letting himself in for. A family that had created a woman like Hannah had to be unusual indeed. They could have continued on to the next coaching inn and squeezed in a few more hours of travel, but why pass up this opportunity? If the woman could tell him more of Hannah, he'd gladly take it, especially after his earlier confession.

He grimaced while he carried the stone up the garden path to the cottage. It was not small by any means, but the long, low thatched roof gave it the appearance of being smaller than it was. Four windows were tucked into the thatch and ivy crawled its way up the side of the white painted walls. The door was painted in a color to match the ivy as were the window frames. It was every inch the sweet country cottage.

His earlier confession…damn, he had not meant to speak so boldly, but there had been something about seeing Hannah up against all those cows, risking her life, that had made him forget all sense. In that moment when he'd had her back in his arms, he had not wanted to let her go.

The truth was, he still did not. He'd told her they would discuss it in London, but what was there to discuss? She lived over one hundred miles from him, wrapped in her bubble of history and research, and was hardly suited to life with a smuggler. He dismissed the idea of his occupation being dangerous and he would never hang for his activities, but that did not mean being married to him would not be risky.

Marriage? Dear God, what had the woman done to him?

A squeal interrupted his thoughts. He peered at the

source of the sound—a tiny bundle of wool topped with a lace crap.

The bundle barreled down the pathway and flung herself at Hannah, nearly knocking the bag from her hand. Hannah laughed and embraced what turned out to be a petite old lady. Ringlets that still held the faintest hint of dark brown poked out from under the cap. Boney hands reached out from the woolen shawl and clasped around Hannah's arms. The woman—her aunt, he presumed—stepped back to eye Hannah.

"I did not know you were coming!" Clear eyes studied her niece, a smile coming across her face as she nodded with approval. "You look well, my dear."

"I am, Auntie." Hannah swung a look at him.

The aunt finally noticed him and lifted a set of spectacles from a pocket deep under the layers of wool and muslin. She did not bother to put them on but peered at him through them whilst still folded. She took her time, and Red attempted to look as gentlemanly and as harmless as possible but he could not help fidget under her intense scrutiny.

"Handsome," Aunt Ellen finally remarked. "Is he your beau?"

Hannah's cheeks reddened. "No, aunt. He is taking me to London."

"Travelling alone with a man, tut, tut." The aunt cackled. "Just like me in my day. I am glad to see your father has not tied you to a desk for your studies and is letting you experience the world."

"I—"

The aunt turned her attention back to him. "What of you? Do you wish to court her? Make her your lover perhaps?"

Red nearly suffocated on his own breath. "No, ma'am. Of course not."

Perhaps the courting bit was a lie. Maybe he lied about

making her his lover too. He wanted both. The aunt was better off not knowing that, however.

"Pity." Aunt Ellen offered Hannah her arm. "Let us get you inside for some refreshments. Will you be staying long?"

Hannah looped her arm through her aunt's. "Just a night if you do not mind."

"Mind? Why should I mind? I do not get to see you enough as it is." Her aunt led her along the path to the front door, and Red followed obediently.

Hannah had been right about the woman not caring about the lack of a chaperone. He'd already known her father did not think much of her travelling about alone, but he could hardly have expected a female member of the family not to object. What an unusual lot they were.

"I will put you in the daisy room," her aunt murmured. "Your friend can stay in the room next to you."

From the slightly mischievous smile on the woman's face, Red suspected the aunt expected him to do something devious like slip into Hannah's room at night. It had not occurred to him until now.

Now it was all he could think on, even as they stepped into the comfortable drawing room, lit by a low fire.

The cottage had feminine touches everywhere which had to mean she had no husband or was a widow. Flowers sat on almost every surface and the curtains were sprigged with tiny flowers in shades of blue. Lace tablecloths finished the look, covering the side tables and the one to the side of a pale blue armchair. A bundle of wool and knitting needles sat on the table, placed in such a way that they looked as though he and Hannah had interrupted quite the knitting frenzy.

"Flora!" the woman called with surprising ferocity. "Flora, dammit."

Hannah grimaced at her aunt's coarse language for which she got a tap to the hand from her aunt.

"When you get to my age, there is little point in airs and graces. Besides, I do so enjoy using colorful language." She grinned at Red, and he laughed.

"As do I, ma'am."

"Good. I am glad to see you are not one of those dandy types."

She urged them to sit down on the sofa opposite. He waited for Hannah to sit and perched awkwardly on the small piece of furniture that had a low back and short seat. Hannah barely fit next to him.

A maid hastened in, her apron smeared with what looked to be jam and her hair dusted with flour. "What is it?" the maid demanded. "I do not have time to—" She paused when she saw the visitors. "Oh."

The maid, though younger than Aunt Ellen could only be five and ten years or so her junior. Her cheeks were rosy with exertion and her black hair, streaked with grey, revealed itself under her cap.

"Forgive me, Mrs. James. I did not know we had visitors."

Aunt Ellen chuckled. "You remember my niece, Hannah?"

The woman finally peered at her. "Oh goodness, of course I do. It has been so long, Miss Hannah. You look so well, and so beautiful. I should have known you would turn out to be beautiful. You grew into your nose then."

"Flora!" the aunt snapped.

The maid clamped her mouth shut while Hannah wriggled awkwardly next to him.

"It is a pleasure to see you again, Flora," Hannah said politely. "May I introduce my friend, Lord Redmere, the Earl of Redmere."

Flora looked ready to faint. She pressed a hand to her stomach and stared at them both. "Goodness."

"An earl, eh?" Aunt Ellen narrowed her gaze at him. "Are you rich?"

He pressed his lips together to prevent a laugh escaping. "Yes."

Elle made a dismissive sound. "Rich men are boring. Are you boring?"

"Not if I can help it," he replied evenly.

"Good. My Hannah needs constant stimulation. She is a clever girl, but I imagine you have discovered that for yourself, have you not?"

He tried not to think of the sort of stimulation he was interested in giving her. Even as she sat next to him, wriggling her little bottom so that it kept brushing up against him, he could feel his mind slipping. It did not matter that the aunt and the maid were present. His thoughts had well and truly sunk into the gutter these past few days, and apparently they were sinking further.

"Some tea, Flora," the aunt demanded. "Tea and cake. A strong man like the earl will be hungry."

He smiled and tried to focus on the aunt's words as she talked of Hannah's father and asked about his latest adventures, but he kept considering how good it felt to have Hannah practically flush against him. Not to mention, they were not usually crammed into a small seat. He could feel every little movement in her body. Including when she tensed as her aunt declared, "Your father is too neglectful of you. I always said to him 'History is not as important as the future. And your daughter is the future.'"

Red focused his attention back on the aunt. He had wondered if anyone else had thought her neglected or whether it was his own assumption.

"I enjoy history, as you know, Aunt Ellen. Father always involved me."

"Unless he was off trekking around the world, digging in the dirt. It is admirable he did not let your sex get in the way of your pursuits, but we all know it was not through choice. He simply does not have time to govern you."

"I do not need governing," Hannah protested.

Aunt Ellen glanced at Red, a slight smile on her lips. "Others would think differently."

Flora emerged through the low doorway and placed a tray of tea and cakes on the side table. Her cheeks were redder than ever and the entire room could hear her huffing and panting.

Hannah's aunt waved a dismissive hand. "Go sit down for a moment, for goodness sakes. No one can hold a conversation with you making that racket."

The maid grumbled and left the room. The slam of a door sounded shortly after.

"Aunt Ellen," Hannah cautioned.

"Oh she will be fine. She likes to lose her temper with me. It gives her something to think about."

Hannah shared an apologetic look with Red, but he shook his head marginally. He was beginning to quite like this aunt.

Aunt Ellen went to pour the tea. Red tried to stand to help, but she motioned him down. "So you are to go to London?"

"Yes." Hannah accepted a cup of tea from her. "You know Father is in France, helping with the recovering of artifacts. We are to take one to London."

"A fool's errand, if you ask me. He would be better off with you rather than risking his safety for some dusty old objects that no one cares about anymore."

"It is not very dangerous," her niece insisted. "And many people care about the artifacts. We cannot let Napoleon steal away history."

"Do you love history?" Aunt Ellen directed the question to him.

"Not particularly, but Hannah is teaching me to."

Hannah looked at him, surprised. "I am?"

"A little," he admitted.

"You are a sensible man then," Aunt Ellen announced. "Do not get your head buried in the books like Hannah's father does."

"There is a little chance of that, ma'am. I am a busy man."

"No doubt." Aunt Ellen's eyes twinkled. "I bet you have many a woman after your hand. And your title, of course. They likely keep you busy."

If she was inferring he was busy bedding his way through all female society, she was wrong, but he hardly knew what to say.

"Red is quite the businessman," Hannah put in. "His work keeps him busy."

"Red?" Aunt Ellen grinned at this. "Red. I like it. May I call you Red?"

"Of course."

"Then you must call me Ellen."

"As you wish."

"Well, I must ensure that useless maid can ready your bedrooms." She pushed out of the chair, and Red and Hannah rose. She waved for them to sit down. "You two enjoy some tea and cake. You no doubt need it." She peered out of the window. "If you need to stretch your legs after your journey, the gardens are a little damp but looking quite fine." She clasped Hannah's hand and gave it a little squeeze. "I am glad to see you, my dear. You look so well, and it is quite nice to see you in handsome company. Your father always did keep company with such dry old sticks."

Hannah pressed her lips together.

"Are your horses being seen to? I assume you came by coach?"

"Yes, Aunt Ellen. We did have Red's private coach, but it

became stuck in the mud. We hired a private coach in Taunton."

"Goodness, what a journey you must have had." Aunt Ellen shuffled to the doorway. "I shall ask Flora to hustle along the stable hand. The lad can take some food out to the men. They will stay comfortable enough in the stables."

"Thank you, Aunt." As soon as she had left the room, Hannah turned to him. "I did warn you."

"That your aunt curses and is quite the naughty old lady? Hardly."

"She was quite the adventurer in her time, I think. Her husband was not the nicest of men. Father spoke several times of her taking lovers. Of course he does not say this approvingly. Once her husband passed away, she became the mistress of someone quite wealthy, though I do not know who. He gave her this cottage."

"She lived for herself by the sounds of it."

Hannah gave a sad smile. "She did, and I do not think she regrets it one bit."

"That is all anyone can ask for, is it not? To live with no regrets. I can only hope we can say the same when we are her age."

Red could not help fear he would have one regret if he did not figure out a solution to his problem. He wanted Hannah, in many, many ways, and if he did not have her, he would regret it for the rest of his life.

CHAPTER TWENTY-FOUR

"These are beautiful gardens." Red strode beside Hannah, taking a casual loop around the lawns with her.

"They are," she agreed.

Autumn was wearing on and the fresh spring and summer blooms were fading, but Aunt Ellen's garden was laid out with paths that wound between trees and ferns as well as some winter plants so as to keep it interesting when there was little color.

However, as beautiful as they were, Hannah rather found the discussion of such matters an odd one to be having with Red. After all, he was hardly the gardeny type.

"I like your aunt," he said finally after doing a loop around a stone statue of Venus coming from her shell.

"She's a character and that does not sit well with everyone, but I like her very much."

"Does she get lonely?"

She shook her head. Her aunt's lover had died several decades ago—or so her father muttered disapprovingly, but Aunt Ellen had never indicated she wanted to have another man in her life. She suspected there were not many men willing to take on a free spirit like her.

"She might bicker with Flora, but they are the best of friends. Flora has been with her since she was a young woman."

"But you do not visit much?"

"I have not seen Ellen since I was—" she paused to think "—about four and ten I think. I suspect my father feared she was a bad influence on me."

"And was she?"

"In some ways, perhaps."

The continued their stroll up to the small orangery at the end of the garden. The brick building was in the style of those that could be seen at estates much like Red's, with long windows and a tall roof but only housed a handful of plants. A small wrought iron table and two chairs sat tucked amongst them.

"Shall we?" Red asked.

She nodded and sat. The weather was still cool and a slight chill had wrapped about her so she welcomed the warmth of the small room, designed to house more exotic plants. The long windows and brick design kept in any heat the building captured.

"Aunt Ellen is a great believer in independence, a hard thing for women to come by. She found it by way of taking lovers, but I do not believe she ever saw them as a means to an end. My aunt is not a planner, so her gaining a roof over her head was mere luck."

"Ah."

"She does not approve of me staying at home with Father. I recall her claiming I would turn into his nursemaid one day."

"Does that worry you?"

Hannah blinked. "I did not think it did. At least not back

then. Of course I was only young with no clue as to what my future held."

"But it worries you now?" He looked at her as though trying to solve a puzzle. His gaze searched her eyes, her face.

She eyed the green frond of one of the plants, tracing the veins through its leaves with one finger. "I suppose." Turning her attention back to Red, she sighed. "I have spent a lot of time looking back, wrapped up in the past. I never really thought of the present or even the future."

"You are thinking of it now, though."

"Yes." The word came out harsh.

"What do you think of when you think of the future?"

You, she longed to say. *A future with you.* But how could she admit to such fanciful notions.

"I suppose...I suppose whether I was to spend the rest of my days running errands for my father or waiting for him to return."

A heartbeat of silence passed between them.

"What would you do instead?"

She licked her lips. Now was her chance. But any words froze on her lips. They all sound ridiculous. *I want to come to Cornwall with you. Be your lover. Be your wife.* She did not care either way.

"Hannah," he said when she did not respond, his voice gruff.

"Yes."

He stood abruptly, and she blinked up at him, unsure what his intentions were. She soon found out. He lifted her bodily from the chair and pressed his mouth down on hers. She found her back pressed up against the brick wall of the orangery. His chest crushed hers. Her eyes were open for the briefest moment, able to see the fierceness and desperation in his face. She closed them once the sensations took over, no longer able to detach her mind from body.

He kept her pinned while his mouth moved across hers. His tongue probed, and she opened her mouth to him, meeting his tongue with her own. She found herself undulating into him, pressing herself against every inch of hardness there was. An ache gathered between her thighs and in her breasts, but no matter what she did, it would not be eased.

Red tore his mouth from hers and stared down at her, panting. His hair was mussed and his lips—saints preserve her—his lips were slightly swollen and all the more kissable. She ran a hand through his hair and down his cheek to feel the rough stubble there. His Adam's apple bobbed.

"Hannah, you drive me wild. How is it you do this to me?"

"I-I—"

He clutched her hand and pressed it between them. She gasped at the feel of his hardness there, pulsing against his placket. She cupped her hand around his arousal to feel the true shape of him, and he groaned.

Red brought his mouth down on her neck, nipping and kissing his way up and down the arch. Sweet frissons swept through her like an endless tide that could not be held back. His hand came up to cup her breast through her stays. She moved into the touch, finally getting a little relief from the desperate ache in her nipples.

She cupped him again, and he darted back.

Hannah flattened her palms against the wall on either side of her. "Did I hurt you?"

"No." He shook his head vigorously. "No. God, it was too good. Any more of that and I would have..."

"Would have?"

"Would have taken you."

She closed her eyes and opened them, lest she was dreaming. Goodness, she should have known that was where it was leading—the ache between her thighs, the desperation for more. Had he continued, she would have let him take her.

"Red—"

He lifted a palm. "Allow me to be something of a gentleman for a change. Let us return to the cottage. You and I being alone is a dangerous thing, I think."

She straightened her shoulders and took his offered arm. There was no sense in being disappointed. Why, it was not as though she could have let him have her in the garden where her aunt could have come across them at any moment. Knowing Aunt Ellen, however, she would probably be immeasurably proud of her niece for taking an earl as her lover.

Aunt Ellen had installed herself back in the drawing room by the time they had returned. Her knitting needles clicked together as she added new row after row of pale pink wool together. She beamed at them. "Did you enjoy the gardens?"

"Yes, they are wonderful. You do look after them well." Hannah sat opposite her aunt, and Red squeeze in next to her once more.

"I have some help of course." She narrowed her gaze at Hannah. "Did you visit the orangery?"

Heat rushed into her face. "Yes." The word came out slightly strangled, and Red shifted in the seat, making her all too aware of his hard thigh pressing into hers.

"You have a bit of fern in your hair, dear," her aunt said, barely looking up from her knitting.

Frantically fumbling for it, Hannah patted her hair. Red came to her rescue and plucked out the bit of plant that must have found its way into her hair when she had been pressed against the wall.

Aunt Ellen peeked up at her, a sly smile on her face.

"Do you mind if I check on the men and the carriage?" Red asked.

She envied him being able to escape.

"Of course. Dinner shall be served in an hour so do not leave us for too long if you wish to change before dinner." Aunt Ellen lowered her knitting. "Though we never stand upon ceremony here."

"Thank you." Red bowed and ducked out of the low doorway.

Her aunt watched the doorway for a few moments giving Hannah a chance to brace herself. Apparently satisfied Red was not going to be returning anytime soon, Aunt Ellen placed down her knitting on the side table.

"Is he your lover?"

"No, of course not." Hannah should not have been surprised by the question and yet she was taken aback still.

"*Was* he your lover?"

"No, Aunt Ellen."

"Have you ever taken one?"

"Aunt, you are obsessed with the idea of lovers. We cannot all live as you did."

"And how is that? You cannot live with fun? With passion? With love?"

"Did you love your lovers?"

A soft small crossed the old woman's face. "Not all of them. I fancied myself a little in love with a few, but I did not love a man properly until my last."

"The man who gave you this cottage?"

"Indeed. He was married though they lived apart. It was a frightfully awful marriage." Aunt Ellen laughed. "When I first met him and he tried to entice me into his bed, I arrogantly told him I could never take just one lover. How wrong I was."

"Did you not worry about your reputation? Did people not give you the cut?"

"A few did but do not forget, my dear, that many rich and powerful men and women took lovers. As long as it was done quietly, few cared as long as they had something to gossip about." She waved a hand. "Enough about me. What of you? Do you wish him to be your lover?"

Hannah opened her mouth and clamped it shut.

"There is no need to be shy, Hannah. You are a strong, independent woman, but you are too tied to your father. It is about time you truly spread your wings. What better way than enjoying some time with your handsome earl."

"I cannot just take a lover," she spluttered.

"Why ever not? Are you saving yourself for marriage?"

"Not really."

"Then there is no harm done. Any man who cares more about the state of between your legs than you are not worth having anyway."

Hannah was beginning to feel a little faint after all this talk. It was all well and good hearing bawdy talk in the inns and even having witnessed the odd naughty tup outside a travelling inn on her journeys, but it was a little different when it was her aunt directing the conversation at her.

"I am not sure I want him as my lover, Aunt."

"Ah." Her aunt pursed her lips. "You love him. You want more from him perhaps."

It was about time she summoned the courage to give words to her feelings. "I think so."

A weight seemed to lift off her shoulders. Once she had uttered the words, the confusing fog vanished. She nodded to herself. "Yes. Yes, I do."

"So you would want marriage and all that?"

"Yes."

Her aunt shrugged. "He seems a good man, but will he stifle you?"

Hannah shook her head. "Never." She twined her fingers together and eyed them. "But it is impossible, even if he feels more than desire for me."

"Oh he does."

She snapped her gaze up. "How do you know?"

"I see the way he looks at you. It is clear as day how he feels for you."

"But even if does...care for me, our lives are very different. He is a high-ranking noble. I am a mere gentleman's daughter. He lives in Cornwall, far from everything and Father—"

"Forget your father."

"Aunt, I love my father dearly. That will not change. Does he not need me?"

"How long has he been away in France?"

"Nearly five months."

"He does not need you, my dear. He loves you, and you love him. That will not change because you are a few hundred miles from each other. That has not changed since he was in France, has it?"

"No."

Aunt Ellen leaned forward and closed her hands over Hannah's own tightly wound together fingers. "You do not need to do your father's bidding to show your love for him. You are a grown woman with interests of your own. I think it is about time you pursued them, even if that means following this earl to the end of the country. If you believe he will support your dreams and desires, then you must take the chance. Cease looking back and start moving forward."

Hannah looked at her aunt's bony fingers, her skin so cold against Hannah's and yet comforting. Did Red truly love her? Would he still support her interests if they married? She supposed he had come this far with her, but she could not forget that she had paid him to do so and this idea of a curse had forced his hand. The only way to be sure, would be to ask him. Maybe she would summon the courage tonight.

Maybe.

CHAPTER TWENTY-FIVE

While the carriage was made ready, they opted for a stroll into the village. Red offered Hannah his arm and they followed a short winding lane to the main bulk of buildings. Just outside of Winchester, it benefited from being so close to the big town in that the merchants only had a short trip to replenish their supplies. The great variety of goods on offer displayed this fact from the drapers to the milliners. Each revealed an abundance of their specialty.

Hannah paused briefly to look in the shoemakers where sets of ladies and gentleman's samples were on display. Red glanced around the village. A few early risers strolled amongst the shops, fashionably dressed, though most of the passers-by were merchant men or servants. A lone carriage rolled down the road with little haste, men on horseback overtaking it as they partook in their early morning exercise.

"There is a subscription library here." He motioned over the road. "Your aunt is well situated."

She glanced up from the shoes. "Oh, that must be new."

Red took her arm once more, and they went to look in

the window. "You rarely see such things in small towns. I should explore if such a thing is viable in Penshallow."

"But you are not much of a reader."

His lips quirked. "You do think me an uneducated lout, do you not?"

"Of course not." Her tone was instantly defensive.

Apparently, after yesterday, he could not tease. Tensions were too high. Even now he felt it running between them. It pounded with his every beat through him, rushing through his veins, whispering to him. *You wanted to take her. You wanted to take her.*

He still did. He had hardly slept at all for wanting her. All it would have taken was for him to slip out of bed, ease open the door, creep across a few creaky floorboards with great care and sneak into her room. That would have been the hardest part. Once he had gained entry into her room, he had little doubt he could have succeeded in drawing her into his arms and seducing her.

"There is quite the library at Redmere House. I confess I have little time to read these days, but I enjoyed many of those books in my youth."

They continued their stroll along the lengths of the road. The yeasty scent of freshly baked bread emerged from the bakers and wrapped about them. He inhaled deeply. Perhaps it would clear his senses.

However, when he glanced down at Hannah who was peering up at him quizzically, he knew there was little chance of that. Her hair had been styled by Flora this morning and although the style was a little old-fashioned, the delicate curls at her neck and the tight drawing back of her hair put emphasis on her features. His attention was drawn to her lips, the arch of her neck, the point of her chin. He wanted to take that chin in hand and draw her mouth to his.

"What is it?" he asked.

"You are a mystery to me sometimes, Red. Sometimes I think I will never truly know you."

"You know me."

She did. She had been the only person in the world to recognize the gentleman underneath the roguish exterior.

"I suppose I do. But you still surprise me."

He grinned. "As do you. I do not think that is a bad thing."

Like yesterday, when she had surprised him with her passion. He had nearly choked on his own breath when she had begun touching his arousal.

Although that could also be considered a bad thing because he had not been able to rid himself of the memory and had spent the rest of the day in a state of half-arousal.

As they reached the chandlery and neared the end of the street, a young man paused in front of them and eyed Hannah. Recognition flickered on his face, and Red felt Hannah stiffen beside him.

"Hannah St. John?"

She nodded. "And you are Barnaby Shaw."

"Well remembered. What brings you to Oakley?"

"I am here visiting my aunt. We are on our way to London."

"Forgive me," he said, finally noticing Red. "Mr. Barnaby Shaw at your service."

Red had taken an instant disliking to him. He could not say way, logically, as Hannah was so fond of saying, but there was something in his keen gaze as it landed on Hannah that made him curl a fist.

About half a head shorter than Red, Barnaby had sandy hair, neatly trimmed and was not unhandsome. With a strong jaw and clear blue eyes, Red imagined he was well sought after by the women. Barnaby's build was a little leaner than his own, but well-cut and tailored clothing made up for that.

Red lifted his chin. "Lord Guy Kingsley, Earl of Redmere."

Barnaby bowed low but met his gaze boldly. Apparently the sound of Red's title had little impact on the man.

"And what of you, Barnaby? What is the reason for your visit?"

"I am here to visit my cousin. She has just recently given birth to a baby boy."

"You shall have to give her my congratulations."

Barnaby smiled. "She shall be pleased to hear of you. You look well indeed."

Hannah arched a brow. "That is not what you said last time we met."

The man's smile dropped. "You must forgive the words of a jilted young man. We are so full of pride at that age."

"You were hardly jilted, Barnaby."

He chuckled. "My heart certainly felt jilted." He looked to Red. "How easily these women may break our hearts, eh?"

"Indeed," Red said stiffly. Jilted? Had they been engaged? Was there some affection? Love? Who the devil was this man?

"How long are you staying in town?"

"We leave before lunch," Red put in.

"Ah. That is a shame. I thought we might be able to catch up. Are your, erm, circumstances still the same? I may address you as Miss St. John?"

Hannah nodded, and Red did not like how the man's eyes sparked with excitement.

"Perhaps we could catch up quickly, before you leave?"

Red made a grunting sound. Christ, he might as well have not been stood there. Barnaby was intent on ignoring him and focusing his full attention on Hannah.

"I am sorry, but we do not have time."

The man's face crumpled a little. "You are still in Alresford, are you not?"

"Yes, my father still lives there."

"I shall have to endeavor to stop by."

"I am sure he would welcome the visit," Hannah said coolly.

"I hope you would too." Barnaby gave her a hopeful smile.

"That is if I am there. I do travel quite a bit."

"Well, I shall take my chance and hope for the best." He lifted his hat. "It was a true pleasure seeing you again, Hannah."

Red bristled at the use of her name. "Come, my dear," he said, his voice overly snooty. "We had better get on if we are to make it to London in time. No doubt there is many there who are eager to see you."

Barnaby gave a quick bow and ducked away, put back by Red's comment. Red hoped the man imagined Hannah had hundreds of suitors in every town and a simple country boy would never be good enough for her.

Hannah chuckled a little as they did a loop back around and strolled down the opposite side of the road.

"Persistent chap," Red muttered.

She sighed. "Yes, he has not changed."

"How do you know him?"

"My Father and his are good friends though he lives on the other side of Winchester. We spent some time together throughout our childhood, and they both came to visit a few years ago. That was the last I saw of him. I'm afraid I rather hurt his pride."

"His pride seems well enough now."

"Yes, it does. I am surprised he even wished to speak with me."

"You did not wish to speak to him," Red stated.

"Not at all. He was quite rude to me upon his last visit."

"How so?"

"He inferred he had romantic feelings toward me. I did not have any for him, however." She glanced up at him. "I tried to be kind, but he did not take it well. He accused me of spending too much time with my nose buried in history books to see what was in front of me then declared no one would marry a bluestocking."

Red winced, fully aware he had called her as much many a time. "Foolish man. He had to have had fragile pride indeed."

"I am well-aware how weak the male pride can be. When your father is involved in study and research, you see them clamor over the prizes and the accolades."

"Come now, we are not all so terrible. I would not relish being turned down by you, but I would certainly never stoop so low as to declare such nonsense."

"You would not," she agreed. "But he was a young, silly man." She peered back to where they had been standing. "I do not think he has changed particularly."

"So you are not interested in him?"

"Not at all."

Relief made his body relax. Of course she was not. Hannah was no fickle creature, yet he could not deny, the idea of her being pursued by anyone else made his skin hot. He had wanted to thrust his fist right through the nearest window when Barnaby had looked at her with such admiration.

"I do wonder if he did not have a point, though," she mused.

"That fool? I am not sure he would know a point if you thrust it in his face."

She laughed. "It is true, though. I have spent much of my life studying and researching. How much did I miss because of it?"

"Hannah, your interest in history is admirable. It is a far

better way of spending your time than playing piano or embroidering cushions. Do not regret that."

"I will always adore history, nothing will change that. I want to know more, always, but even my aunt expressed that I have missed out on much because of following my father about." She pursed her lips. "I wonder, sometimes, about the places I have been. I hardly remember them except for what we went there to study."

"There is no reason you cannot change that."

"Yes," she agreed.

A quiet bubble of hope began to boil in him. Hannah wanted life to change. She could have no idea how courageous it was of her to admit as much. The majority of men and women, Red had discovered, loathed change. They would do whatever they could to keep things the same, even if it was against their own interests. Few had the courage she did.

And if she wanted her life to change, he could offer her the biggest change of all. But would she really be willing to be with a smuggler and take on all the risks that came with it? Even her inferior rank did not concern him. He had no father to impress any longer, and he cared little for what anyone else though. The local people would probably be pleased he had picked someone of lower rank.

Good God, he was gone. He had fallen entirely. He wanted to marry this bluestocking and take her home to be a smuggler's wife.

They made their way back along the lane toward her aunt's cottage. He felt as though he were walking in a daze. Something inside him had twisted and changed. He was a new man, excited for a future he prayed he could get. His life had been about the present and little else. When their next shipment would come. Could they avoid the excise men yet again? How would he disperse the goods? Whilst he had accused Hannah of looking back too much, he had not been looking forward at all. He had lived in stasis for too long.

He narrowed his gaze at the approaching man—one of the footmen, he realized. A heavy weight came to rest in his stomach. What now?

"One of the horses has thrown a shoe, my lord. We will have to get him reshod."

The weight in his gut lifted. "Do you think your aunt will mind if we stay an extra night?"

Hannah beamed back at him. "Of course not."

A foolish grin worked across his face. Another night with Hannah. Maybe he would broach the subject of him courting her tonight.

Maybe.

CHAPTER TWENTY-SIX

I *would not relish being turned down by you.* Hannah tossed to one side. *I would not relish being turned down by you.* She shifted onto her back, the soft mattress no more comfortable than a bed of rock. Why had she not picked up on him saying that before? Had he said it flippantly or with true meaning? Had it been a hint as to the depth of his feelings? Could they possibly be as deep as hers?

She eyed the cornicing on the ceiling, the swirls faintly visible thanks to the light seeping in through the gap in the curtain. The night had proven clear and bright, with a multitude of stars freckling across the sky. She had spent a good hour or so staring at them until she had given up and retreated to bed.

She found no rest there, however. Instead her mind had suddenly latched on that one phrase of Red's.

I would not relish being turned down by you.

If that were true...

Hannah huffed out a breath and closed her eyes. If that were true, there was nothing she could do about it now. He was abed, and it had to be past midnight.

The encounter with Barnaby had been a blessing really. She recalled their last meeting when he had followed her about like a little lost dog. He was not at all interesting to her, and she suspected he only liked her because he seldom had female company. In spite of being mildly attractive, he did not have the charm to make female friends.

When he had asked to court her, she had turned him down as politely as she could. Goodness, she had only been young and certainly not interested in men or boys. Unfortunately, his response had reflected his lack of charm and had only sealed her impression of him. The insults he had thrown at her of being bookish and a bluestocking had dented her pride a little, but the words had been hurtful enough for her not to consider that there might have been truth behind it. Bluestocking, yes. Bookish, indeed. But this idea of her missing out on things had failed to register.

Until recently.

Until Red.

This journey—this wild, inconvenient, uncomfortable journey—had opened her eyes. Her thoughts were no longer merely on the stone but on other things, like what would she do next, what could her next accomplishment be? What would bring her happiness in life?

She was fairly certain being at Red's side. Whatever he offered, she knew life would never be dull with him.

Exhaling again, she pushed up to sitting and snatched a robe her aunt had lent her. Slinging it around her shoulders but failing to do it up, she trudged downstairs and out of the rear door to the gardens.

The night was not cold, but it touched her skin like cool silk, refreshing her. Underfoot, the grass was dewy. She wriggled her toes into it. When she peered up at the sky, more stars appeared. The moon was not even a half crescent as though stepping aside to let the stars have their moment.

She stared up at them until her neck hurt then strolled down to the orangery.

The trees about her rustled, and she stilled. A bat swooped out of one, flying in a loop before vanishing and reemerging with a second. Hannah pressed a hand to her heart and laughed at herself.

"Something funny?"

She whirled, keeping that hand to her furiously beating heart. It only took her a moment to register the baritone that sent a shiver down her spine.

In only a shirt and breeches, Red was in as much of a state of undress, entirely inappropriate for strolls around the garden, but perfect for midnight walks when one could not sleep, she supposed.

"What are you doing out here?"

She eyed his tousled hair and absorbed the sound of his slightly gritty voice. "I could not sleep."

"Why?"

Somehow she suspected he wanted more than a mere shrug of an answer. His gaze was on hers, unwavering. "I was thinking," she said softly.

"As was I."

"Of what were you thinking?" she forced herself to ask.

His gaze flickered down to her chemise. It was not the first time he had seen her in one, but they had not very nearly made love before. Now the significance of a mere slip of fabric covering here skin was monumental. Neither of them could ignore her peaked nipples or how his gaze heated. How she could even sense that in the cool starlight, she did not know, but there was something in his slightly hooded eyes that told her he was not thinking of the beautiful night or the peaceful setting.

He was thinking of what was under her chemise, just as

she was considering how much she longed to touch that firm, warm chest.

"Pardon?"

Hannah blinked. She could hardly recall what she had just said herself. "O-of what were you thinking?"

"I forget now," he said. Red moved closer. "I forget." He reached for her, and she swayed into him. "Christ, Hannah, you make me forget all sense."

She fit so perfectly against him it stole her breath.

He cupped her face. Against the starry night sky, he was perfect—a stark contrast of humanity against the magical.

"You make me forget all..." He scowled and searched for the word.

"Logic?"

"Yes."

"Me too."

"What does your gut tell you?"

She hardly had to think about her response. "That I want you to kiss me."

He groaned. "Your gut has never been so right."

Only the briefest moment passed before he lowered his mouth to hers, but it was too long. She moved onto tiptoes to close the gap more quickly. He gave her no quarter. This was no gentle teasing kiss. There was no consideration of her inexperience, and for that she was grateful. Red saw her as a woman to be desired and nothing more or less. He kissed her as though she inspired the sort of passion that was only written about.

Hannah wound her fingers into his hair, faintly aware of the soft silkiness. His hands gripped her face tight. He kissed her deeper, stole her breath. Desperation seared her. It was not enough. Would it ever be? She moved her body against him and searched for release, but there was none to be had.

She skimmed a hand down his back and slipped it under his shirt.

Rewarded with the feel of smooth, warm skin and his muscles tensing beneath her fingers, she moaned against his mouth. Red released her face and used his hands upon her back to flatten her against the arousal that was pressing against his placket.

"What do you do to me?" he groaned when he briefly released her mouth.

"The same as you do to me I think." Her voice hardly sounded like her own. It belonged to another woman. A wanton, desirable woman who was finally taking what she wanted from life.

He pressed back her hair from her face with one hand, keeping her close to him with his other hand on the base of her spine. "Hannah, I cannot resist this time. You have weakened me."

"I do not wish for you to resist."

"There is something you must know first."

She gulped. "What is it?"

"Before I take you, you should know..." He blew out a breath.

"Red," she pressed, exasperated, hardly able to keep herself still in his hold. She pressed a reassuring kiss to his jawline.

"You should know that I have fallen in love with you, Miss Hannah St. John." His lips were quirked into a tilted smile as though he could not quite believe it had happened. She was not sure she could either.

Mouth ajar, she stared at him, searching his eyes for some sign that he was fibbing or teasing her. She had hoped, of course, and dreamed too. But being faced with the reality of a man like Red loving her was more than she could comprehend. She wanted to take a moment to study him, to take in his words and analyze them. Spend a few days studying what it was between them and think logically on it.

Of course, no such thing could be done and love could not be studied or looked at logically. That was something she had slowly begun to understand.

"Hannah?"

The worry in his eyes was quite charming but she would not let him suffer. She rallied her courage with a deep inhale. "You should know, Earl of Redmere, that I have fallen in love with you too."

The smile that broke across his face quite charmed her. He kissed her firmly, holding her to him as though making sure she did not try to change her mind.

Well, there was little chance of that.

"I don't know how it happened," he said. "How did you do it?"

She gave a secretive smile. "We bluestockings have our ways."

"If every bluestocking in England is like you, we men are sorely missing out. Yet I have my doubts. I know with utter certainty there is no woman like you, Hannah."

"For a rogue, you do have a way with words."

His grin turned wicked. "I have a way with touches too."

"You do?"

"I do." He eased his grip on her for a moment. "If you do not wish this, you must tell me now, because when I touch you, I lose my head."

Hannah remained silent. He grinned and kissed her again. For how long their lips and tongues met, she did not know. All she understood was it was the most satisfying and unsatisfying moment of her life. She was kissing the man she loved and he loved her in return, but she needed more. When would he give it to her?

Red's hand crept between them while he scattered kisses

along her jaw and back to her mouth. Her lips felt plump and swollen from his attentions, and her body tingled from head to toe.

A hand curved over her breast, and she could have sworn she nearly swooned.

"Red," she murmured, urging him on. He pushed her robe from her shoulders and pulled the lace holding the neck of her chemise cinched around her shoulders. Whilst he kissed her fervently, his hand slid beneath the cotton. She shivered at the contact.

Red tore away and eyed his hand upon her breast. "I cannot take you here." His hand, however, said differently, playing over her skin and toying with her aching nipple.

"We cannot sneak back into the house. Aunt Ellen will surely hear." She glanced at the orangery. "There is a chaise in there. Will that be..." She gasped as he tweaked her nipple. "Will that do?"

"It will." He released her breast, kissed her forehead and took her hand.

Inside the orangery was darker than outside, but enough starlight seeped in through the long windows for her to find the chaise tucked at the back of the building, slightly hidden behind several plants. She eyed the chaise with trepidation. She had seen sex once or twice, usually up against a wall behind an inn, and of course animals cared little for whether or not they had observers, but she did not think either way looked enjoyable.

She twined her hands together and dropped her gaze. "I know it hurts. I understand," she spilled out.

Red chuckled and took her hands to press kisses to the back of each one. "It does not need to," he said.

She lifted her gaze to his.

"Hannah, I promise it does not need to, but you need to understand this. I am going to spend a long, long time preparing you. I am going to bring you so much pleasure that you will think you are utterly spent. Then I will bring you more. If I have to spend the rest of the night making you ready, I will because I would rather die than hurt you."

"Oh do not say that. Do not speak of death."

"Fine. I will speak of your pleasure, though." He nodded to the chaise. "Sit."

She did as he bid, and he came to kneel in front of her. Red pushed up her chemise and settled between her legs. He set one palm on her thigh and used the other to urge her forward. She held her breath, feeling stiff and useless.

"Relax," he murmured, touching her lips with his.

His kiss melted her tensions. She forgot her inexperience and recalled how desirable he made her feel. His fingers twined into the steadily loosening braid trailing over her shoulder. As he kissed her, the hand on her thigh worked up and then inward, moving ever closer to her sex. She could not help but rock her hips forward.

"Impatient girl," he said with a grin.

He kissed her deeper this time, twining his tongue with hers while his fingers traced the crease of her thigh then higher, connecting ever-so-gently with her folds. She jolted. He groaned into her mouth. Red's fingers upon her most private parts were entirely unlike her own. She felt more sensitive, more aware.

He stroked her gently before becoming bolder with his movements. She could hardly concentrate on kissing him back so he released her mouth, supported her with a hand to her neck and scattered kissed across her shoulder and neck.

His fingers did not enter her as she supposed they might do. Instead he stroked and circled over and over. Hannah moved with him, finding a unique rhythm that had the pleasure building quicker than she could have thought. He flicked her nub several times then went back to circling it. The pleasure broke slowly—one bright burst that seemed to go on. She shuddered in his arms as he slowed the pace.

"I am not sure who found the most pleasure there."

She lifted her head from where it had been resting on his shoulder. "It had to be me surely?"

He shook his head. "Watching you orgasm is quite the sight."

She nodded. She hoped she would get the chance to see him do the same before the night was over. Maybe he would teach her to pleasure him.

"Spread your legs and lie back," he ordered softly.

Too dazed to question the command, she slid back and parted her thighs. He lifted the chemise, baring her to the night air. Her mouth grew dry at the desire in his eyes.

Then he lowered his head.

"Red?" she asked, her voice strangled.

"You will still be sensitive," he warned. "But I will be gentle."

His hot mouth upon her juncture nearly made her bolt up from the chaise. She threw her hands wide and gripped the edge of the chair. He started gently, as promised, licking carefully along her crease. As she settled into it, he grew bolder, swiping his tongue up her before circling and sucking at her nub. It hardly took her any time to reach her peak, and she came hard against his mouth.

Panting, she pressed a hand against her damp forehead. He looked up at her with a smug grin. His hand slipped between her legs and he used the other to tug down her chemise and reveal one breast.

Her eyes widened. "Not again, surely?"

He nodded and brought his mouth down on her breast. He nibbled on her nipple, making the sensations in her body multiply. When his fingers connected with her sex again, she was hardly sure she could take it yet she was boneless and unable to do anything other than accept another orgasm.

When he did it again, he pressed his fingers into her. She arched into the touch. Relief coursed through her. This was what she had been craving, and it did not hurt one bit. He moved two fingers in and out of her before adding a third.

"Now?" she asked.

"Demanding woman," he teased and stood. "Yes. Now."

He tore his shirt over his head, revealing that wide chest covered with a scattering of dark hair that she had thought of many a time since his illness. Then he tugged off his boots and pulled down his breeches. She remained with her legs spread, so wanton, she could hardly believe this was her, and yet she could not care.

Her gaze landed on his arousal, thick and long and surrounded by dark hair. Her body gave a pulse of recognition. This is what you want, her body told her.

"Take me, Red," she begged.

CHAPTER TWENTY-SEVEN

R ed could not claim to be a saint. He'd seen many women naked and in many different states. However, nothing had ever had such an impact on him.

Hannah lay, her legs spread, her sex glistening and visible to him. Her eyes were heavy lidded and her lips puffy. He had left a few red marks on her breast where he had nipped her. It was not possible for his cock to get any harder, but if it had been, it would have lengthened at the sight of the starlight shimmering across her bare skin.

He moved slowly. He had never fallen prey to the thought that taking a woman's virginity made him special or tainted her in anyway, however, there was an element of pride in the idea that he was her first.

And her last, if he had his way.

Boneless and at his command, she let him move her to lie properly on the chaise. He knelt between her legs and hooked both thighs over his hips. The painful desire surging through him urged him to thrust deep into her, but he gritted his teeth and fought it.

"Hannah?"

She gave him a slow, satisfied smile. "Take me, Red," she urged again.

He smiled. She was relaxed and ready, exactly as he wanted her. He'd been told by too many women who painful their first time was, how that was the way it had to be. Not with him, damn it. He would not be one of those fools who thought of only his own pleasure.

He bent to kiss her and pressed a hand beneath her head. "Look," he urged.

She peered down between her legs and gasped. His erection was not even an inch from her.

"Keep looking."

He shifted forward, his blood pounding fast through him when the head of his cock touched her damp folds. He pressed in slowly, watching her face for any sign of pain. Her mouth opened at the sight of their joining, but she did not stiffen or wince.

She closed about him like a warm, velvet glove. He closed his eyes for a brief moment urged her to relax back. Her fingers curled around his shoulders. He kissed her before rocking out and back in. She released a tiny mewling sound that wrapped about his heart.

The rhythm took him eventually, sapping him of his control. Hannah panted in his ear and rocked with him. He felt her body pulse about him, so near the edge already. He thrust hard into her while the pleasure burned through to his very soul.

When she came, it was more dramatic than he could have imagined. She gasped his name and spasmed about him. Jaw tight, he moved in and out of her while scattering unsteady kisses across her face. Her nails dug into his back. The bliss peaked. He withdrew quickly and spilled across her stomach. He pumped his cock with his hands a few more times and gave one final groan.

Sweaty and out of breath, he sat back against the chaise and stroked a lazy hand against her thigh. Who would have thought lovemaking with a bluestocking could be so life changing? He met her gaze and took in her satisfied expression.

"You really are a rogue," she murmured. "A gentleman too," she added.

"And you are a beautiful, sensual woman." He wiped her off with the sleeve of his shirt and kissed her forehead. "And a bluestocking. *My* bluestocking."

Red recalled why he loathed London as soon as the carriage entered the outskirts of the town. Horses, carts and coaches clogged the roads and smog lingered over the buildings, coating them with a fine blanket of dust. It took them a good hour to make their way to Bloomsbury where the British Museum was situated. Hannah twined her fingers through his and he eyed her pale gloves against his dark kid leather ones. She offered him a smile that made him want to kiss her firmly.

The previous days had become a blur—but the most pleasant blur possible. He made love to her whenever he had the chance. And Hannah...damn, what a woman she was. When he had first met, he could not have possibly predicted such a passionate woman resided under that uptight bluestocking exterior.

They neared the museum. He peered out of the window at the grand facade. Consisting of one long stretch of a building, lined by two wings and covered in tall windows, it occupied a huge amount of space in Bloomsbury. They entered through wrought iron gates onto an entirely cobbled front.

"Have you ever been here?"

He shook his head. "Never had the occasion I'm afraid."

"They have quite the collection these days. They opened up the Department of Antiquities not long ago."

Red nodded vaguely. He could not claim to be overly interested in the exhibitions. Mostly he was looking forward to getting the stone off his hands. Then he could concentrate on what he really wanted his hands on.

She narrowed her gaze at him. "Red," she warned, likely well aware of what he was thinking.

"Yes?"

"Stop it."

"I am not doing anything," he protested, adopting an expression of utter innocence.

"Yes, you are."

"And what, pray tell, was I doing?"

"Thinking," she hissed.

"And a man is not allowed to think?"

"He is. But not of things like that."

"So I am to never think of you ever again?" He leaned in. "I am to never think of your beautiful body? Or how you flush the most wonderful pink color when you orgasm?"

That same color appeared on her cheeks, and she batted his hand away. "Fine. Just do not do it so obviously."

"I shall try my best."

The coach came to a stop outside the front door. It was ajar, inviting visitors in. Red did not know much about the museum, but he had been aware that since its opening it had been free to visit for those of an inquisitive nature and that the collection had grown into one to be admired by many.

He'd rather admire Hannah.

Climbing out of the carriage, he aided Hannah down, and she adjusted her bonnet and smoothed her skirts. A little nervousness was clear in the slight shake of her hands. He gave them a little squeeze and spoke with the driver.

"I'm not sure how long we will be. You may wish to find a nearby coaching inn and return once the horses are cared for."

The driver nodded. He had already made the man aware they were to return to Taunton at the first opportunity and would be paid handsomely for the return journey. After that he would request his private coach to meet him in Plymouth. Hopefully he would have Hannah accompanying him, but they had yet to discuss it.

In truth, they had yet to discuss much. Each time he got her truly alone, he found it hard to do anything other than kiss her. They had remained wrapped in each other's arms most nights, and they talked of history and smuggling and fathers and brothers and aunts. But never about their future.

He wanted a future with Miss Hannah St. John. He just needed to ask her for it.

Once that blasted stone was gone, then he would ask her. He did not much wish to risk such a question whilst still in possession of that bad luck charm.

The carriage made a turn around the courtyard. Hannah made a frantic motion. He scowled and approached her.

"The stone," she said. "Red, where's the stone?"

"Blast."

The carriage was already making its way out of the gates. He sprinted after it, running directly into a woman wearing a hat that appeared to be made entirely out of feathers. She held said hat and blustered about rude men. He muttered an apology and hastened up the street after the coach.

"Stop," he shouted, drawing the attention of everyone but the driver. "Damn it."

He barged through the crowded streets. There were plenty of other horses and coaches spilling into the street from side roads which slowed the coach, but he was unable to be heard over the din of conversation and rattling wheels and the clop of horse hooves.

He came alongside the carriage and shouted to the driver again, but he ignored him, likely not even realizing the bellow was directed at him.

Red forced his way farther forward, ahead of the coach and pushed out into the street. Breath held, he waved his hands frantically at the driver, hoping he would actually see him. Distantly he heard a woman scream. It sounded like Hannah.

The driver spied him and brought the coach to a frantic halt. Red took a few steps back and gulped down a breath. He waved at the interior of the vehicle. "Forgot...something..." He opened the door and retrieved the stone before motioning on the coach that was aggravating many a driver and rider.

He twisted only to nearly slam into Hannah.

"What were you thinking?" she demanded.

"That we needed the stone?" He hugged the artifact close to his chest.

"You could have been killed!"

He shook his head. "I knew the driver could stop in time. After all, I am paying his wages."

"Honestly, Red, you need to spend less time thinking with your gut and more time using your head."

He flashed her a grin. "My gut works perfectly, thank you. It led me to your bed," he whispered.

"You are incorrigible."

"And you love me for it."

She shook her head and laughed. "That I do."

They headed back to the museum and entered through the open front door. It was no different to any other stately home, which surprised Red though there were some impressive and likely old statues occupying the hallway. Black and white tiles covered the floor, and his and Hannah's footsteps echoed across it. Elegant marbled columns rose to the high ceiling, and a staircase of marble covered in red carpet led upstairs.

Hannah guided him through the state rooms, each housing collections of parchments and vases and other antiquities that he hardly had time to admire as she paced ahead. He smirked to himself. Perhaps she was rubbing off on him. He could never claim to have had any interest in a few dusty old vases before.

They came a stop outside a closed door that had *offices* painted on in gold lettering. Hannah knocked and waited, practically hopping from foot to foot. The door opened, and a young man with a smooth jaw and carefully swept aside black hair peered at them.

"Miss St. John!" He beamed at them. The man was likely a couple of years younger than Hannah, but that did not prevent appreciation flickering in his gaze.

"Good afternoon, Richard. Is Sir Melbourne here?"

"He is indeed." The whelp of a man grinned. "We have been expecting you. Your father sent on word that you were to be expected with the find." He uttered *the find* as if it were some magical object. "I believe he was in the Department of Antiquities. I shall go and find him for you." A slight hint of color sat on the man's youthful cheeks as his gaze ran up and down Hannah. "He will be pleased indeed you are here. As am I, of course."

"Thank you," Hannah said, apparently oblivious to Richard's admiration.

"Am I to fend of every intellectual within a five-mile radius?" he muttered to her.

"Pardon?"

"Richard, if I am not much mistaken, is quite enraptured by you."

"You are mistaken. He is three years younger than me, for one."

"Men love older women."

"Do you?"

He liked the little spark of jealousy he saw there. It made a nice change. He had never considered himself the jealous or possessive type, but he had encountered two men who were clearly half in love with her within the space of a week and that was two men too many as far as he was concerned.

When Richard returned, he was out of breath but still took the time to ask after Hannah's health and completely ignore Red. An older gentleman followed shortly after, his smile warm. His skin was the dark hue of a sailor that suggested he spent much time in hotter countries. The curling white moustache decorating his lips stood out in stark contrast to his skin and was stained with tobacco around his top lip. His full head of matching white hair was in disarray, fulfilling perfectly the image of a preoccupied intellectual who had little time to worry about his appearance. The only thing that did not match that was the moustache that had been waxed to perfection.

"You have it then?" the man asked, ignoring Red once more.

He was beginning to get used to the bloody stone being more important than him.

Melbourne opened the office door and motioned to a desk covered in papers. Red paused, unsure where to place the artifact amongst all the chaos.

"For goodness sakes, Richard," Melbourne spluttered. "Clear some space."

The young man hastened forward and swept the papers aside, spilling some onto the floor. No one seemed to care. All eyes were on the artifact as he laid it down and pulled open the fabric covering it.

Utter silence. Hannah, Richard, and Melbourne stared at the object. Red could hear his own heartbeat. He glanced at Hannah who was spellbound. Lord knows why because she had spent enough time studying it.

Melbourne moved forward suddenly, and Richard jumped a little at the sudden movement. Melbourne ran a finger along the text and let out a heavy breath.

"This is…"

Hannah nodded excitedly.

"It will change so much," Melbourne continued.

They all nodded apart from Red who merely watched the exchange with a raised eyebrow.

"What we will learn…" the old man breathed. "This." He waved his finger at the stone. "This will be the greatest find of the century, mark my words." He clasped her hand. "You, my dear, have done your country—no, the world—a great service."

"Well, it was really down to Lord Redmere here. I could not have done it without his aid."

The man seemed to finally see him. "Of course, of course." He shook his hand vigorously and with surprising strength for an old man. "We shall have to dedicate something to you both. A room perhaps or a bench."

Red shook his head. "I need no thanks." And he certainly did not relish the thought of people placing their arses on a bench named after him. "It was Miss St. John's passion that ensured the safe delivery of the stone. She deserves any accolades."

"Your father will be thrilled." Melbourne turned his attention back to the stone, drew out a quizzing glass and peered at it.

"Will you send word to him for me, Sir Melbourne? I will not be remaining in London for long." Hannah gave him a soft, slightly hesitant smile.

"Yes," Red agreed. "We have much to attend to." He smiled back at her.

"Oh there is no need. We received a letter from him some five days ago. He is due to return to London in two days' time," Melbourne said, still bent over the stone.

"Oh." Hannah chewed on her bottom lip.

Oh indeed. Red's stomach sank. So much for his plan to take her back to Cornwall and marry her forthwith.

The old man smiled. "You shall be wanting to wait for him, I have no doubt."

"Yes, I suppose I will."

Melbourne tucked away his quizzing glass and straightened. He frowned and patted his pockets. "I cannot for the life of me recall what I did with the letter, but he mentioned something of a new expedition. It sounds as though he could do with your assistance."

Red's stomach dropped entirely out of his toes and vanished. How could he compete with that? Christ, he would not even ask her to choose.

She stilled and glanced at Red. "I see. Did he say he would stay at the George Inn?"

"Yes, I believe so."

Hannah nodded. "Well, I shall leave you to your studies. I look forward to hearing what conclusions you come to."

Melbourne chuckled, his moustache twitching with the movement. "It shall take many years of study, I suspect, but we will get there. Thank you again for your assistance, my dear. And of course you, my lord."

They bid the men farewell and stepped outside. The carriage had not yet returned, and Red doubted it would be back for another hour yet at least.

"You will want to stay in London then," he said, his voice sounding hollow.

"Yes, I must speak with Father."

"I see."

"Red, why do you look like that?"

"Like what?"

"As though I have just stolen your favorite toy?"

He shook his head. "I cannot wait in London. I must return. I have been away too long, and it's unfair to leave the men any longer."

Her throat bobbed. "I see."

The rattling of wheels on cobbles drew his attention from her. The stable hands at wherever the coach had stopped must have been efficient indeed.

The carriage came to a stop, and Red climbed up to grab Hannah's bag. He handed it over, and she stared at it for several moments.

"Do you need me to take you to the inn?"

She shook her head, a crease appearing between her brows. "No. But Red—"

"I am glad I could be of service. It was an interesting journey to be sure." He was blathering like an idiot, but if he was not careful he would beg her to come with him and how could he? How could he ask her to give up what she loved doing most for a life as a smuggler's wife?

She drew up her chin. "I owe you some money, I believe. For the dresses."

"Consider them a gift." And perhaps she would think of him every time she wore them.

"Red," her voice cracked.

He took her in his arms and held her close, feeling his heart slowly splinter apart. He had known it as soon as Melbourne had uttered the words. She likely knew it too. They could not be together, not when the world was out there for her to explore with her father.

For many moments, he savored the feel of her warm and

soft in his arms before pushing her back and kissing her forehead. "I wish you every happiness, Hannah."

"But, Red, you can—"

"Must make haste," he muttered. "Much to do. I have certainly spent far too much time away from home."

Her expression grew pained. "But I thought…" She shook her head. "Red, why can you not—"

"Farewell, Hannah." He cut her off for the second or third time, unable to bear the pain of her telling him she would choose her father over him.

He climbed into the carriage before she could utter a response. He shut the door and did not peer out until he had tapped on the roof and they began to move off. Her face was a picture of confusion, and he saw her mouth something. Red looked away and focused on the empty seat opposite. A little niggling voice told him she had said *stay*.

CHAPTER TWENTY-EIGHT

Rain hammered against the windows and wind whistled through the gaps in the panes. The fire in the library sputtered in protest as a gust whipped down the chimney. Thank the Lord the ship had docked during the day when the weather was better. They would bring their haul once the weather improved. Red snorted. It would not have been logical to bring the barrels in tonight.

He swilled his brandy around the glass and pushed it aside. Alcohol held little appeal tonight. Or any night since his return. His gut was telling him something. Telling him he was wrong. He should have given Hannah the choice—him or history. But he had been a coward. Because it was easier for him to walk away than to listen to her say she had chosen history.

Some roguish smuggler he was.

The doorbell echoed through the house, ringing on and on through the quiet rooms. If that was Nate, he would throttle him. He hardly needed to ring the bell.

When no footsteps sounded, Red forced himself up and stomped through to the hallway. It was late indeed but he would have expected the butler to be around at least. He would probably be reading one those blasted gothic novels he was so fond of and was entirely absorbed. Red was going to have to ban the damned things from the house.

He hauled open the door, ready to see his brother, soaking and with some excuse for not being able to open a door himself.

He froze. Blinked several times. Peered closer. His heart near cracked his rib cage as it jumped.

"Hannah?"

She gave a weak smile. "C-can I come in?"

He opened the door farther and ushered her in. The rain had glued her pelisse to her and her bonnet was a soggy mess of ribbon and straw. A curl had wrapped itself about her face and was sticking to her lip. She pushed it aside.

"What the devil are you doing here?"

She undid her bonnet and clasped it tightly. "That was one awful journey," she said with a smile.

"I cannot be any worse than ours."

"Oh it was. You were not with me for one." She gave a little shudder.

The fragile movement sparked him into action. "Come on through, we had better get you dry."

"Not the first time I have been soaked through in your company," she chattered.

He led her through to the library and pushed one of the chairs in front of the fire before handing her his discarded brandy. "Drink up, it will warm you."

She took a sip and clasped the glass between both hands. "T-thank you."

"What are you doing here, Hannah? And why the devil were you out in this weather?"

"The mail coach stopped by the harbor. I had to walk from there."

"You should have stopped at the inn."

She shook her head.

Red leaned against the fireplace and took in the sight of her. Even a soggy mess, she was beautiful. He had missed looking at that stubborn chin and those long-lashed eyes. Missed kissing those lips too.

"Why are you here then? Is something wrong? Christ, are you—"

"There is nothing wrong. Well, there is I suppose, but not physically or in any other way." She gave a shaky smile. "When you left London, you did not give me much time to speak, or even think. I hardly knew what had happened."

"It was for the best," he muttered.

"Was it?" Her smile grew bolder. "I had this feeling, right here, in my gut." She pressed a hand to her stomach. "At first I thought that, logically, you had changed your mind about me. That perhaps you loved me but not enough to want anything more from me. It made sense. You are an earl, after all, and you had said nothing of our future together. But the more I thought on it, the more my gut told me that was not right."

Red hardly wanted to ask the next question in case the answer was not what he wanted. "What did you gut say then?"

"It said that you did love me. That you did want me. It said that for some reason, you ran away."

"I did not," he grumbled.

"Yes, you did." She stood and set the glass down on the mantelpiece. "You ran away, Red. You, the bold, brave smuggler ran away. It hurt me very much."

"Christ."

"I thought to let you go for a while until my father came to London. He wanted me to come to an island off the Highlands of Scotland. They are digging up a medieval village there."

"Why are you here then?"

"When I listened to my gut, I knew I did not want that. Before I met you, I would have followed my father simply to spend more time with him, but I would have merely been hanging on his coattails. I need to do something on my own terms."

"So you came here to tell me you are heading off somewhere alone? Is that why you came?"

"No." She stepped closer. The fire smoothed her skin and warmed her complexion. It turned her eyes almost amber. The agonizing need to kiss her burned through him.

"No," she repeated. "I know what I want to do on my own terms."

"And what is that?" His voice came to strangled.

"I want to be with you. And I think you want to be with me."

"But your passion for history...for all of that. I could not get in the way of that." He swallowed the giant knot that had gathered in his throat. "That is why I ran. I did not wish to get in the way of it."

"That is what my gut told me." Hannah reached up and pushed a lock of hair from his forehead. "But you will not get in the way of it. You helped me with the stone, and I know you will support me in whatever I endeavor to do." She grinned. "There have been a few wonderful fossils discovered in the Cornwall recently. I thought I might be able to turn my attention to that."

"So you did want me?" he asked, hating himself for how weak he sounded.

"Yes. I merely wanted to speak to my father and let him know that I would be going to Cornwall with you. I doubt he would have objected to me marrying an earl, but I had to tell him in person." She cupped his cheek. "I still want you. And I think you want me too."

"What does your gut say?"

"It says you do."

He wrapped his arms about her and pinned her to him. "Damn right I do. I was ready to bring you here and marry you in an instant. I still am. God, forgive me for being a fool."

"Oh, Red."

"I think if you had not found me, I would have come to you. Hell, I would have followed you to the Highlands and played escort again if I had to."

"And given up smuggling?"

"Absolutely."

"Well, there is no need for that."

"You are prepared to be the wife of a smuggler?"

"I certainly am as long as you are willing to be the husband of a fossil hunter."

"I would not have it any other way."

"And the husband of a bluestocking?" she teased.

"And the wife of a rogue."

"And a gentleman," she added. "All of it. I want it all."

Red could hardly take the words in. He grinned foolishly but could resist no longer. He took her mouth in a long, heated kissed that was only broken by the sound of the front door slamming shut.

He took Hannah's hand. "That must be Nate. Come let me introduce you as my fiancé."

Her beaming smile made his heart warm. Perhaps the stone had not been cursed, after all. All the trials it had put them through had brought them to this point. One day he would visit the damned thing again and thank it.

He led her back to the entrance hall. His brother was shaking off his hat and a woman stood behind him. Red recognized her as Miss Gray, the daughter of a local gentleman.

"Nate, you remember Miss St. John?"

"Ah." His brother dipped his head, rain droplets spilling from the shoulders of his greatcoat onto the marble floor. "I do indeed. Whatever are you doing back in Cornwall?"

Hannah glanced at Red.

"Hannah has just this moment agreed to marry me."

Nate laughed and took Miss Gray's hand. "What a coincidence. So has Patience."

The End

Find Samantha on her website
www.samanthaholtromance.com

Made in the USA
Middletown, DE
18 May 2020